BOOK of legion

Skulls & Lace

ja huss

BADLANDS MC
BOOK 5

Necessary Reckoning.
Spectacular Collision.
Brutal Reality.

Time to burn it down, boys.

Purgatory is over.

Book of Legion - Badlands MC #5
A Dark Outlaw Biker Serial Romance
SKULLS
&
lace
New York Times Bestselling Author
JA HUSS

SKULLS AND LACE

Copyright © 2026 by JA Huss
Cover design by JA Huss
Interior design by JA Huss
ISBN: 978-1-957277-64-6

Necessary Reckoning.
Spectacular Collision.
Brutal Reality.
Time to burn it down, boys.
Purgatory is over.

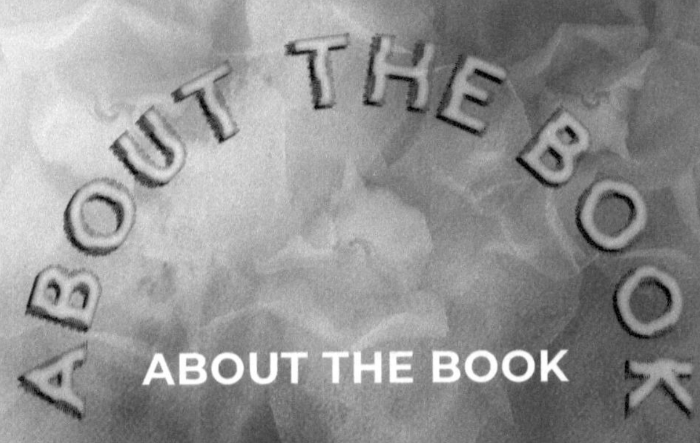

ABOUT THE BOOK

Their love story has always been impossible—ranch heiress and outlaw biker, angel and demon, the girl in white dresses and the man covered in biblical warfare tattoos.

Savannah's life is content. Her engagement to a senator's son is brand. Everything has been managed, controlled, and performed to perfection.

Legion's life is hell. His family was destroyed long before he was born. His ending predetermined long before he met the Little Ashby Princess in a silo.

They've been stealing moments since they were teenagers, burning for each other in a world that keeps demanding they choose sides.

Now it's time.

Necessary reckoning.

Spectacular collision.

Brutal reality.

Time to burn it down, boys.

SKULLS AND LACE

Purgatory is over.

Inside the pages you can expect:
🏍️⛓️🔥 Outlaw Biker Romance
💎🖤🔧 Rich Girl / Poor Boy
⛓️🔒🖤 Property Of
🖤🔪 Morally Gray / Anti-Hero MMC
🔥👁️⛓️ Obsessed / Possessive MMC
🚫💚 Forbidden Love
💍🖤 Only Her
🖤🔪 Only Him
💕🏠 Childhood Sweethearts
🔪🔪💀 Touch Her and Die
🔥🌶️ Primal Spice
🔒🖤 Secret Relationship

LEGION

CHAPTER 1

LEGION

The clubhouse door hits the wall as I shoulder it open, the familiar smell of cigarettes and spilled beer doing nothing to mask the iron tang of blood. Blood on my hands. Blood on my shirt. Blood trailing behind us like breadcrumbs through the fucking forest. One month back with my brothers, and already everything's gone to shit.

"Move!" I shout, kicking a chair out of the way as Crow and Dusty struggle through the door behind me, Butch's weight sagging between them. His head lolls forward, chin touching chest. Too much blood loss. Too much time in the truck getting back. The prospects' faces are ghost-white under the fluorescent lights, eyes wide with panic. Kids playing at being outlaws until the bullets start flying.

"Jesus fuck," someone whispers from the bar.

"Not helping," I growl, scanning the room. Too many eyes watching. Too many mouths that'll talk later. "Everyone out. Now."

The bar empties in seconds—hangarounds and weekend warriors all scrambling for the door. Only patched members remain, frozen in place like they're watching a movie they can't pause.

Butch groans, a wet, rattling sound that means there's blood in places it shouldn't be.

"Put him down," I order, clearing empty bottles and ashtrays from the closest table with a sweep of my arm. "Here. Don't rock him, Dusty! Be careful!"

The prospects lay Butch down, his body heavy and unresponsive as he bleeds out on the table.

I've seen enough gunshot wounds to know this one's bad. The entry wound is a small. A nice, neat hole just below his collarbone. But the exit wound is a ragged crater of flesh.

His skin is gray, his lips blue at the edges.

Fuck. He's not gonna make it. He's not gonna make it.

"Where's the fuckin' doctor?" I demand, pressing my palm against the wound. Blood seeps between my fingers, warm and steady.

Crow shakes his head, swallowing hard. "I've called him three times. He didn't pick up."

"Try again," I snap, meeting his eyes. "And keep trying until he does."

Crow nods, stepping away with his phone pressed to his ear.

"What happened out there?" Ledger asks from somewhere behind me. "That route was supposed to be clean."

Clean. That's almost funny at this point. I reach for clean bar towels, packing them around the wound.

"Ambush. Three trucks came in, no lights on. Like they had night vision. They knew exactly where we'd be. We were in the middle of the drop, piling it up under the tarp behind the gas station on Route 12, when they came burnin' in. Butch had to abandon his bike and hop in the damn truck. That's how he got shot."

"What did they take?" Diesel asks.

"All of it," I snap. "All of it, Diesel."

"Well..." Roach shrugs. It could've been a coincidence."

"Bullshit," I scoff. "This is the third time this month something's gone sideways." I press harder on Butch's wound, and he groans. "Someone's feeding information. We've got ourselves a fuckin' rat."

The room goes quiet except for Butch's labored breathing and Crow's desperate voice in the corner, still on the phone.

"Got him!" Crow shouts. "He's twenty minutes out."

"Tell him to make it ten," I order.

Diesel meets my eyes, sighing. He knows it's true. Things are... not OK here in Badlands. Haven't been since I got back. "Let me take over," he says, pushing my hands away from Butch's wound. I let him do it because I'm so fuckin' pissed, I might explode if I don't walk it off.

Diesel places his big hands over the towel that's already wet with blood while I play the ambush on a loop in my head.

We were loadin', then... we heard them. But it was fast. There was no time to get out. Then the lights flashed, lit up in three directions. They started shootin' immediately.

I cannot even believe that Butch was the only one shot. At least a dozen bullets went whizzin' by me, missin'. But just barely.

I'm lookin' at the clubhouse door, still lost in the memory, when it swings open and Brick walks through.

Well… finally. "Where the fuck have you been," I snap. "I've been callin' you for twenty fuckin' minutes." I point at Butch on the table.

Brick approaches, unhurried. Like our guys bleed out on tables every day of the fuckin' week. "Church at noon," he deadpans. "We'll discuss." He doesn't even look at Butch. Doesn't ask what happened. Doesn't offer to help.

What the fuck is happening here? "Did you hear me? I've been callin' you. We were ambushed. Someone knew the route."

Brick's face remains impassive. "Bad luck."

"Bad *luck*?" I echo, incredulous. "Three times in a month isn't bad luck, Brick. It's a fuckin' pattern."

Brick's eyes go narrow. "Are you tryin' to say somethin' here, Legion?" His voice is dangerously soft.

The room goes still. Diesel's hands remain steady on Butch's wound, but I can feel the tension radiating from him. Everyone is watching. Waiting to see what I'll say.

Not everyone is happy these days. I've heard lots of grumbling over the past few weeks. Lots of questions about Brick's new attitude. And all the 'bad luck' as he calls it.

Maybe not half, but close to half of the patched members are starting to think… maybe we need a new leader. Maybe Brick's time has come.

Diesel would never go against Brick. Ever. But…

he's not happy, either. And if the men put it up for a vote and his name came out on top, he'd step up. I know he would.

Problem is, we've already got a fuckin' Prez.

And he's been the Badlands Prez for nearly twenty years now.

That's a lot of earned allegiance. A lot of history.

But that shit runs out quick when you start making mistakes like this.

So I pull myself up to my full height and narrow my eyes right back. "Yeah. I'm doin' more than just sayin' something here, Brick. I'm questioning why our prez doesn't seem concerned that one of his brothers is bleedin' out after a setup."

Brick's expression doesn't change. "As I said, church at noon. We'll discuss it then." He turns, like he's just gonna walk out.

"We need to discuss it *now*," I press. "Someone sold us out. Someone who knew the route, the timing, and the exact location of the exchange."

Bricks stops. Kinda side-eyes me over his shoulder. "And you think you know who, do ya?" The challenge in his voice is clear.

I take a step toward him, hands sticky with dryin' blood. "I think it's interestin' that comms went down right before the ambush. I think it's interesting that you weren't on the channel when we called for backup." Another step closer. "Where were you, Brick?"

The silence that follows is absolute. No one breathes. No one moves. It's the kind of silence that precedes violence—the moment before a storm breaks.

Brick's eyes go dead. "Careful there, Legion. You're a

baby patch around here still. No one cares about the thirteen fuckin' years you wasted as a prospect doin' God knows what. In fact, what the hell were you doin' all those years you were here, but not. You were one of us, but not."

"Well, I know where the fuck I was for three of them."

"Ah, right," Brick sneers. "Your fuckin' prison time. My God. If I had known that you'd canonize yourself for three short years in the hole, I'd have chosen someone else to take the heat. You never shut up about how you did time for us. Even that fuckin' whore sister of yours had to mention it when she was at the gate holdin' her shiny, new Ashby baby." Brick turns to look at the club. He throws up his hands. "Am I right, or what? Raise your hand if you're sick of hearing how Legion sacrificed for us."

No one raises their hand. At first. But as Brick waits, they realize… he's lookin' for support here. He wants to know who's still got his back. And he's takin' notes.

Lots of hands go up.

Diesel's doesn't.

Brick looks at him, chortles. "Come on, Diesel," he says. "You're sick of it too. You've said as much."

I don't look at Diesel. He's allowed to have his own opinion. And sometimes people say shit just because they feel like they have to.

Like most of the members in this room right now.

I know damn well Dusty and Brick do not get along. Dusty is about ready to call it quits. After being here almost eighteen months as a prospect, he's ready to say fuck the Badlands patch, pack up his woman in the laundry, and try his luck with another club farther west.

But his hand is up.

I don't look at him, because I know Dusty now. And the regret he feels for playing along to Brick's bullshit will show all over his face if I look him in the eye.

Men do what men gotta do.

But that don't mean that some of these guys wouldn't have my back if it came down to it.

Brick looks back at me, his anger stowed, but present. "Remember who brought you in, Demon. Because it's the same man who can put you out."

We stand there, locked in a stare that says more than words ever could. Three weeks ago, I would have backed down. Three weeks ago, I still believed in brotherhood above all.

"Doc's here!" Crow calls from the door, breaking the moment.

Doc Simmons shuffles in, medical bag in hand, reeking of bourbon. His eyes dart between Brick and me, sensing the tension but wisely choosing to ignore it.

"Move," he orders, pushing past me to reach Butch. "Everyone back. Give me space."

Diesel and I step away from the table as Doc begins his work, muttering to himself as he cuts away Butch's shirt.

Brick turns without another word, walking toward the back hallway that leads to his office. His shoulders are relaxed, his pace unhurried—a man without concerns. A man certain about his place in the world.

I stay behind, watching as Doc works on Butch, barking orders at the prospects to fetch water, towels, his spare kit from the truck. The blood pools on the table, drips to the floor, spreading in a dark stain across the concrete.

I look down at my hands—red and sticky, already drying at the edges. Then back to the door where Brick disappeared.

The math isn't complicated.

The conclusion isn't pretty.

The danger isn't coming from outside. It's coming from in here.

We got ourselves a rat.

And right about now, as I study the room, I realize I'm not the only one who knows who it is.

I count eleven faces starin' at the door where Brick disappeared.

Eleven is good, but not nearly enough.

I push through the clubhouse door, escaping the smell and the chaos of a brother down and on his way out. Dawn's breaking over the eastern hills, streaks of orange and red runnin' across the horizon.

I fish a cigarette from my pocket, gettinn' Butch's blood all over my pants. I light up, drawing deep, letting the smoke fill the hollow spaces where trust used to live.

But as I look around the parking lot, I realize… there are bikes here I've never seen before. I missed them on the way in because of Butch and the sun was still sleepin'.

But there's no way to miss it now.

I recognize Hammer's custom paint job. Reaper's extended forks. Ghost's blacked-out Road King. The others belong to men whose faces I've seen but whose names I've never learned. New blood that came in while I was up at Whitefall.

These bikes are lined up in perfect formation on the far side of the parking lot. Not in line with mine, or Diesel's, or any other bike that actually belongs here. But alone. Apart.

They all have chromed wheels catching the first light, leather seats beaded with morning dew. Engine's still tickin' from the ride in.

Nobody rides in at 5 AM unless they're called. If you don't live on site, there's no real reason to be here on a random Tuesday at dawn.

Unless someone *did* call them.

All this calculation happens in the span of one exhale. On the inhale, I see them. Four men over by Ratchet's garage, leanin' against the door. Smokin', watchin' me through narrowed eyes.

Their cuts are fresh. Their boots, too.

I nod. None of them nod back.

I circle toward my Dyna, moving casual. My eyes trace the bike, checking for loose wires, for any sign someone's been at it. Nothing obvious, but that doesn't mean shit. A man who knows what he's doing can make a bike fail in a hundred invisible ways.

I turn, inhale again. Exhale. Think.

Three runs in a month gone sideways. Three times we've lost everything because we got hit.

Each time, Brick assigned *me* point position.

Each time, the routes changed last minute.

Each time, comms failed right when we needed them.

Movement catches my eye—a flash of blonde in the

clubhouse window. Brandy, with her phone pressed to her ear, watching me with those empty doll eyes. She doesn't look away when I catch her. Just keeps staring, keeps talking into the phone.

I take another drag, letting the smoke burn my lungs.

From behind, I recognize Diesel's footsteps. "So… church," he says, stopping beside me. "Noon. Everyone's bein' called in."

I exhale smoke. "Yup."

"What did I tell you." Diesel's voice is carefully neutral as he turns to look at me. "There will be a next time, member that?"

Of course, I remember that.

"This is 'next time', Legion. I sure the fuck hope you're ready. Because you will not have thirty-nine members with you today."

The silence stretches between us, loaded with everything we're not saying. The last full church ended with eight members voting against me. Eight members who thought Savannah was a liability. Eight members who will have a say at noon about whatever the fuck is happening here.

"Who are these guys?" I ask, nodding toward the line of motorcycles.

Diesel's jaw tightens. "Nomads from out west."

"Nomads?" I frown. "Since when? I've never heard about any nomads."

"That's because you were doin' time, Legion. They came in about… oh, two years ago, maybe."

"Came in? What's that mean? What are you sayin' here?"

Diesel looks at me, scoffin'. His words drop low, almost a whisper. "What the fuck do you think I'm sayin', Legion? Think about it. New guys, new bikes, new cuts. And not a one of them ever came in as a prospect."

So it's true. Brick is a rat. He's sold out. For protection, or money, or both. And these… nomads. They're Feds. Brick is workin' for the fuckin' Feds.

"They're gonna get a vote today?" I ask.

Diesel grunts. "You've got me, I'll make it clear no matter the cost." He says it quiet enough that only I hear. "But I don't know how many of the others will stand with us."

"They all know?" I'm floored.

Diesel takes a drag, blows out smoke. Nods, just enough so I can see. "They know."

Fuck. Infiltration two years ago. And Brick just… took the whole club along with him? That's what these fuck-ups were about. Me. The new patch.

Brick needs me on board. So he made sure I'd go along by settin' me up to take the fall.

"We didn't have a choice," Diesel says. Already reading my mind. "There were a lot of fuckin' threats. But I've been taking precautions. Lots of us have. And I'm done with this bullshit."

He drops his cigarette, stomps on it, and walks away.

I glance back at the clubhouse where Brandy still watches from the second-story window.

I drop my cigarette too, crushing it under my boot. The sun's climbing higher now, burning away the morning mist, but doing nothing for the chill that's settled in my bones.

The club doesn't feel like mine anymore. Maybe it never was. The brotherhood I thought I was joining, the family I believed I'd found—it's all smoke and mirrors.

A pretty lie told to keep me in line.

I look back at the clubhouse, at the strangers watching me from bikes and windows. The noose is tightening. I can feel it around my neck, pulling snug with each passing hour.

This isn't paranoia anymore. It's survival.

My phone buzzes against my thigh like a wasp. I know who it is before I pull it out. Seven-thirty. Like clockwork.

Mercy's morning check-in.

I step away from the line of traitors, putting distance between myself and whatever trap is being laid, and swipe open the message.

Morning! Library day today. The librarian says I can have FIVE books this time because I brought the others back early. This uniform ITCHES though. Eliza says we should put fabric softener in the wash but I don't know what that is. Miss you!

A photo follows. Mercy in her Rimrock Academy uniform—navy blazer with the school crest, plaid skirt, white button-up. Her hair's pulled back in a neat ponytail, not the wild tangle it was when I first came home. She's standing on stone steps, backpack slung over one shoulder, smiling like she's never been hungry or afraid.

Clean. Safe. Standing tall.

I stare at the image longer than I should. Somewhere in the back of my mind, I register the sound of motorcycles starting up. Men moving around the lot. But I can't look away from her face—the Kane eyes, our mother's smile. All the good parts without the damage.

Walking away from her was the right choice. The only choice.

I send my standard response: Thumbs up emoji and a black heart

Words would break something. If I started typing what I really feel, I'd never stop. And what good would that do either of us? Better she has this clean break. Better she believes I'm just an asshole who left, not a dead man walking into whatever Brick has planned.

My phone buzzes again. Second message.

Savannah said to tell you 'hi' this morning.

I don't answer this one at all.

Instead, I slide the phone back into my pocket, its weight grounding me.

Because while it was a bit of drama after I left, Savannah is, above all, an Ashby.

Proud.

Confident.

Not the kind of woman who pines over a man who decides to leave.

But also, not the kind of woman who turns down a fuck at the silo, either.

LEGION

CHAPTER 2
LEGION

Our hookups resumed after Savannah and I broke away from each other. That's just how it is with us. We are something separate. Not meant to be together for real, just allowed stolen moments at midnight if we're brave enough to take them.

Dust and flowers.

I got there first. Just like I used to when we were kids. The silo rose up like a monument to every sin we committed inside it.

That worlds will shake if we should truly touch,
Yet still we meet in this forsaken place.
The desert blooms conceal what costs too much—

Being there, inside the silo, always felt like somethin' sacred and sinful at the same time.

Where crimson stones bear witness to our sin,
And thorny flowers bloom from pain and such
Forbidden longings burning from within.

And that's what we are. That's what this is.
Our love is Purgatory.
An endless space of nothingness.

This wasteland keeps our secret, dark and grim—
A place where damnation and light begin.

Nothing but cravings, and dead hope, and forbidden fruit.

It was always like that with Savannah and me. Her angel to my demon. Her rise to my fall. Her light to my dark.

Dust and flowers.

This is the only way it works. She stays in her Heaven, I live in my Hell. And as long as we abide by this one rule—this one commandment from God—*do not eat the fruit…*

The world still turns.

But the moment we taste it—not the sin of fuckin'. That's not the forbidden part. The moment we take more than was offered, the moment we reach for happiness in the same space—the world just spins apart. Spirals out of order like a dirt devil on the desert sands.

That night, last week, my motorcycle was outside, cooling in the night air. And even though she was the one who demanded this meeting via text, I had myself half-convinced she wouldn't come.

But she did. Hoofbeats echoed through the night, announcin' her arrival.

Moments later, Savannah appeared in the doorway, just a silhouette back lit by the moonlight. She was wearin' a white sundress, almost glowin' as she stood there in the dust. No makeup. Hair flowin' down her shoulders. The girl from before, not the woman I left behind.

But her eyes—they burned with something that wasn't there when we were young.

She didn't speak to me, not right away. She just came inside like she always did. Though nothin' about this night was like the ones that came before.

We circled each other like wolves, neither of us willing to break first. Her bare feet made no sound on the concrete. My boots echoed with each step. The space between us felt electric, charged with everything we couldn't put into words.

"Three weeks." She broke first. "Three fucking weeks, Legion."

I didn't answer. What could I possibly say that wouldn't sound like an excuse?

"You just disappeared. No note. No call. Nothing." Her voice was loud, crackin' at the edges. "I woke up and you were gone. Like you'd never been there at all."

"Come on, Savannah." I kept my voice flat. "You know who I am. You always have."

"I knew who you were," she spit back. "Not what you'd do."

"And what did I do that was so fuckin' surprisin'?" The anger rose inside me. Hot and familiar, but out of place in the presence of Savannah Ashby. "You got what you wanted."

She scoffed at me. "I got what I wanted? How the hell do you figure?"

"You got Mercy. I don't know why you and your family are so fuckin' interested in mine, but she was the goal, wasn't she."

"I am interested in her because of you!"

"Oh, that's the part I do understand."

"What are you talking about?"

"You're just like him, ya know that? Deep down." It was a lie, I knew that. Savannah isn't nothin' like Cash. But I felt it in the moment, so I said it. "Mercy isn't just a charity project, she's your tether to me."

This made her laugh. "My *tether* to you? I don't need a tether to you, Legion Kane. I *own* you." She looked me in the eyes when she said that, serious as a fuckin' snake bite. "I own every bit of your heart. I don't have to conjure up a fake relationship with your baby sister to hold your interest. I live rent-free in your diabolical mind every moment, of every day."

She wasn't wrong.

"I saved her," Savannah stepped closer to me with her chin raised. "While you were unconscious with sepsis, Cash was filing for emergency custody. What was I supposed to do? Just hand her over?"

"You should have asked me."

"When? While you were dyin'?" Her laugh was bitter. "Or after, when you were too busy acceptin' my hospitality to take notice?"

We're close enough now that I can smell her perfume. Something expensive, with notes of vanilla and amber. It makes my chest ache.

"You wanna tame me," I told her. "You wanna undo everything I've built in my life."

"What have you built?" she snapped back. "You're a biker in an outlaw club, Legion. That's not a foundation for anything!"

I didn't take the bait. "You just wanted to fix the broken Kane kids, like we're another Ashby project."

Her eyes flashed. "That's not true."

"Isn't it? You got what you wanted. Mercy in your fancy academy. Me in your mansion. Everything nice and contained where you could manage it." I didn't have to throw in the dig at the end—but I did. "You're just like your mother."

Her self-righteous indignation reared its wild head so fast, I almost laughed.

"Like my *mother*?" At this point she was hissin' at me. "I wanted us safe. All of us. Together."

"But on your terms."

"Better than yours," she growled back at me. "What was your plan? Steal her away so Cash could sic the sheriff on you? Send his dogs to hunt you down? Go back to the club that didn't want either of you?"

The truth of it burns, even in the here and now. But I didn't flinch. "You don't get to decide what's best for us."

"Someone has to." Her voice dropped. "Since you're so fucking determined to destroy yourself."

"I chose the only family that ever wanted me."

Her laugh was cruel. "Family? The same family that branded you like cattle and let it get infected?"

"At least they don't pretend to be something they're not."

"And what am I pretendin' to be?" Her voice trembled when she asked this.

"Someone who wants me for *me*." The words tasted like ash. "Not just another broken thing you can fix to heal whatever your mother did to you."

Her palm cracked against my cheek before I even saw it coming. The slap echoed in the empty silo, sharp and final.

But I caught her wrist before she could pull away. Instincts, I guess. I held it between us like evidence. "You don't get to walk away from this," I told her in a low voice. "Not until we finish it."

"It was finished when you left," she whispered, but she didn't pull away.

For a heartbeat, we were suspended in that moment —her wrist in my hand, her eyes locked on mine, both of us breathing hard with things we couldn't take back.

Then we just… collided.

It was something out of a movie, I remember thinkin'. An uncontrollable moment of her mouth crashing against mine, her teeth scraped my bottom lip hard enough to draw blood. I pushed her back against the silo wall, pinning her there with my hips.

She bit down on my lip, and I growled into her mouth, my hands already bunching the white fabric of her dress, pulling it up her thighs.

"I hate you," she gasped into my kiss, even as her fingers tore at my belt. "I fucking hate what you did."

"Show me," I challenged her, sliding my hand between her legs to find her already wet. "Show me how much you hate me."

She made a sound like she was breaking and shoved me back, just enough to create space. Then she was workin' my jeans open, yanking them down my hips with none of the tenderness we typically share.

I ripped her panties down her legs, the delicate fabric tearing in my hands.

"You left me," she accused, wrapping her hand around my cock, stroking hard enough to hurt. "You just walked away."

I silenced her with my mouth, pushing her harder against the wall. The silo was cold, but we were burning up. Her hand twisted around me, demanding, punishing as she jerked me off. I slid two fingers inside her, feeling her pussy clench around them.

"Fuck you," she breathed, even as she rocked against my hand. "Fuck you for making me want this."

I lifted her up, hands rough on her thighs, and she wrapped her legs around my waist. Her nails dug into my shoulders, breaking the skin, as I pushed her against the wall.

"Is this what you came for?" I asked, positioning

myself at her entrance. "To remind yourself what it feels like to be fucked by a demon?"

"Shut up," she hissed, and then pulled me into her with her heels against my back.

I fucked her hard, without gentleness or restraint. She cried out, head falling back against the metal wall with a dull thud. Her white dress was bunched around her waist, already stained with dirt from the wall and my hands.

"This what you need?" I demanded, driving into her with each word. "To be fucked against a wall by someone who ruins everything he touches?"

"Yes," she gasped, her nails drawing blood from my shoulders. "Yes, goddammit."

We weren't making love. We were tearing each other apart.

Her teeth found my neck, biting down hard enough to leave a mark. I gripped her thighs tight enough to leave a bruise, holding her up as I pounded my cock into her.

"Tell me you don't think about this," I growled against her ear. "Tell me you don't wake up wet, thinking about me inside you."

"Every night," she admitted, voice breaking. "Every fucking night."

I shifted my angle, hitting deeper, and she threw her head back with a cry that echoed through the empty silo. Her body tightened around me, so close to the edge.

"Come for me," I commanded, one hand moving to where we were joined, finding her clit with my thumb. "Come while you're thinking about how much you hate me."

She fractured around me, her body convulsing, walls clenching around my cock as she cried out my name like it was torn from her throat.

I followed her over, emptying myself inside her with a groan that sounded like surrender.

For a moment, we stayed locked together, breathing hard, sweat cooling on our skin. Her legs were still wrapped around me, my face buried in her neck. Neither of us spoke.

There wasn't nothin' left to say that our bodies hadn't already confessed.

Finally, I lowered her to the ground. Her legs shook as she stood there, and she didn't look at me when she pulled her dress down.

The white fabric was smeared with dirt and sweat, torn at one shoulder where I grabbed her too roughly.

I fixed my jeans, watching her. She moved to the small mirror she hung up years ago, trying to smooth her hair and wipe away the evidence of what we did. But there was no hiding it.

She didn't speak as she walked to the door. Didn't even look back.

Outside she whispered something to Cassia, then it was nothin' but hoof beats.

I stayed behind, sitting on the concrete floor where we first kissed when I was sixteen. My body was spent, but my mind was racin'.

This wasn't over.

It was never going to be over between Savannah and me.

The silo had always been our confessional. Our battlefield.

Now it's our purgatory—the place we return to punish each other and feel alive.

To remember what we lost and what we can't let go.

I knew she'd be back.

And so will I.

Back in the here and now, I stare at the text from Mercy, my thumb hovering over the screen. *Savannah said to tell you 'hi' this morning.*

"Hi" isn't a greeting—it's a summons. It's the sound of a match being struck.

It's code. Not something we ever agreed on, but it's Savannah's way of callin' me to the silo.

Meet me tonight. Fuck me tonight.

That's what 'Hi' means.

I rub my thumb over the screen, feeling the brand on my chest throb with my heartbeat.

I blow out a breath, wishin' this day was already over.

Waitin' until midnight will be torture.

I glance back at the clubhouse. The whole place is a powder keg. Brick's selling us out. He wants me to join in. Accept whatever deal the Feds are offerin'. And if I refuse, he wants me dead.

And none of it matters when I read that text.

Hi.

I should tell Savannah no. I should focus on figuring out what I'm gonna do. I should be sitting with Butch, or planning my next move.

But I know exactly where I'll be at midnight.

Same place I've always been when she calls.

Same place I'll always be.

Because when it comes to Savannah Ashby, I've never known how to say no. Not at sixteen. Not at thirty-two.

She is my poison fruit and I will never stop tasting her.

I light another cigarette, inhaling deep enough to burn. The nicotine doesn't calm me anymore, but the ritual gives my hands something to do besides reaching for her ghost.

I type out a reply to Mercy, delete it, type again. My finger hovers over the send button.

Focus on school. I'm proud of you.

It's the only clean truth I have left to give. The only part of me that isn't stained with blood, or lies, or broken promises.

Everything else is scorched earth. Club politics. Brothers who might be enemies. Brick's calculating eyes. Butch's blood drying under my fingernails.

And Savannah. Always Savannah.

I hit send and crush out my cigarette under my boot, calculating how long I have to wait to feel her wet pussy clench around me.

Then I turn back toward the clubhouse, already feeling her skin under my hands, already hearing her breath catch when I push my cock inside her.

Some men pray for salvation.

I just count the minutes until damnation.

CHAPTER 3
SAVANNAH

I sit at the breakfast table, running my finger around the rim of my coffee mug. It's seven-twenty. The silver spoons clink against porcelain. The staff move silently around us, refilling coffee, removing plates. Every sound echoes in the high-ceilinged dining room. Every movement feels choreographed.

I didn't want to come down this morning. Didn't want the food or the forced conversation. But here I am anyway, because that's what Eleanor trained me to do. Breakfast at 7:15, dinner at 6:30. Family meals aren't optional. They're religion. They're law.

"More coffee, Miss Ashby?" Miss Charlot asks.

I nod, not trusting my voice. The dark liquid pours, steam rising like a spirit escaping. I watch it curl and vanish.

Cash sits at the head of the table—Eleanor's chair. He's reading something on his tablet, barely acknowledging me. Three weeks since Legion walked out. Three weeks of this pantomime of family.

Wyatt stumbles in, twenty minutes late and riding some chemical high. His eyes are too bright, pupils pinned. Cocaine, probably. Could be pills. With Wyatt, it could be anything—he never did have any self-control. At least he showed up. As soon as Legion left, Wyatt came back to the family table like a vulture returning to a carcass.

"Morning, sunshine," he drawls at me, dropping into his chair. His hand shakes slightly as he reaches for the coffee.

I don't answer. Just take another sip from my mug.

The emptiness to my right is what gets me. That's where Colt always sat. My brother, my confidant. The one person in this house who actually saw me.

And now he's gone. Off with Destiny and the baby, somewhere out of reach and out of touch. Somewhere with a new life that doesn't include any of us.

I can't blame him for escaping. I just wish he'd taken me with him.

But the silence he left behind is deafening. There's no one to catch my eye when Cash says something particularly pompous. No one to kick me under the table. No one watching my back.

I feel his absence like a phantom limb. An ache where something vital used to be.

And then, the new emptiness—the absence that Mercy left behind. I never expected to miss a nine-year-old girl I barely knew three months ago. But I do. I miss her questions about everything—why the chandelier has exactly twelve crystals, why we have three different kinds of forks, why the horses get turned out twice a day.

She brought something to the house that hasn't been here in decades.

Innocence.

And sisterhood, in a way. Growing up with three brothers never gave me that softness. The boys were all competition, and protection, and testosterone. But Mercy was different. She made the ranch feel less like a museum exhibit and more like a home.

Less like a cage.

Now she's at Rimrock, and the house echoes with her absence. I find myself listening for her footsteps on the stairs, expecting to see her burst into a room asking about dinosaur bones, or horse anatomy, or whatever new obsession she'd developed that day.

And not even Puddles can make up for it. Though the puppy misses her dearly, too.

Surprisingly, it's Cash that Puddles looks to for attention now. Not me. And he allows it. Hell, he's embraced it. Says the dog has the breeding to be a proper retriever and is planning on taking him duck hunting this fall.

So... again. As always... it's just me and my horse against the world. Even more so now. No Mama, no Colt.

No Legion.

Just empty spaces where people used to be.

My phone lights up with a notification.

I tap it open immediately, grateful for the distraction. Rimrock Academy is trying out a new AI system this year that sends thirty-second "magic moment" clips each morning—snapshots from the previous day. They call it "parent portal glimpses."

I'm not her parent, but I'm on the approved list.

Small miracles in a time of self-destruction.

I watch as Mercy walks between classes, her uniform crisp, her backpack bouncing slightly. The camera catches her in the library, bent over a book with intense concentration. Then talking with Eliza, her assigned "sister"—a fifth-grader who started as a school requirement but has become something real. They're laughing about something, heads bent together over a shared secret.

I see the changes in her already, subtle but unmistakable. Her shoulders aren't as tense. She smiles easier now. There's a confidence in her stride that wasn't there before. She's becoming a different child from the one I knew at the old trailer—the one who was taught to shoot and 'check sixes' by a gang of outlaw bikers.

A Cinderella story, if Cinderella had a tattooed brother and a messed-up family history.

I watch the video twice more, happiness and longing tangling in my chest. Would Mercy hate it if I stopped by to say hi? It's not like I have a job or anything important to do. I manage the Ashby social accounts. I post pictures and videos of perfect moments that never actually happened. That's my sole purpose in life when the Kanes aren't in it.

I don't want to bug her or make her feel 'watched'. That would be the worst. But I miss her. And not just because of the way she brightened the ranch up, but because she's my connection to Legion.

Mercy and I talk every night—we catch up every evening, at least until she replaces me with a gang of giggling schoolgirls. It should be enough, but it's not. Last night I asked her to tell Legion I said "Hi."

Just that. Just "Hi."

But between Legion and me, it's code. It means: I'll be there tonight. I'll wait thirty minutes at the silo. If you show up, we can fuck.

This is how it's always been between us. Little messages that appear out of nowhere. Subtle signals that mean I'm thinking of you. I want to see you. Come see me tonight.

I wonder if he'll show. I wonder if he's still angry.

Not gonna lie, the hate fucking is amazing.

The first time, anyway.

But I don't want to hate-fuck him forever.

I want to love that man so hard. I want to be his everything.

Thirty minutes at midnight will never be enough time to say everything I need to say with my body, since words always fail us.

"You're quiet this morning," Cash says suddenly, watching me too carefully over the rim of his coffee cup.

I don't answer him. Just sip my own coffee and stare at the window, where Montana stretches out forever, vast and empty and full of places to hide.

Cash sets down his cup with that practiced precision he does everything with. The gesture itself is a performance—the way his pinky lifts slightly, the way he places it exactly in the center of the saucer. Everything Cash does is calculated, even when no one's watching.

"The cattle auction's next week," he says, not looking

at me directly. "You will be there, right, Savannah? It's time to choose bloodlines for the coming year."

I stare at my plate, pushing eggs around with my fork. The yolks have congealed into a cold, rubbery mess, a metaphor for my life.

"We've got those Wagyu-Angus crosses to consider," he continues, as if I've shown any interest. "And that new bull from Calgary—"

"I know how the auction works, Cash."

He clears his throat, folding his napkin into a perfect square. "Well. It's good you're here for it. Especially with everything that's happened." His voice shifts, adopting that patronizing tone he uses when he thinks he's being insightful. "Legion being gone... it's a good thing, Savannah. For everyone. Mercy's safe now. You're back where you belong. This was the right call."

I don't respond. Don't agree. Don't even look at him.

The silence stretches between us like a living thing until Wyatt snorts from across the table. "Right call," he mimics, voice slurred slightly.

It used to be that Wyatt would make an attempt to hide his addictions. Back before Eleanor died. Now, he just doesn't care for the pretense, I guess.

"Like that Kane girl's gonna turn out any different than her trash brother or that knocked-up sister." Wyatt's laugh has always been a mean sound with no humor in it. "She's a lost cause. Just like all of them. Demons and whores—"

"You would know about lost causes, wouldn't you, Wyatt?" My voice comes out quiet, precise. Not angry. Just... factual. The table goes still. Some wounds don't need volume to bleed. "How many times has Cash paid off your dealers? How many rehab centers have kicked you out?" I set my fork down carefully. "If it wasn't for me managing this family's image, you'd be another homeless addict shooting up under a bridge somewhere. Another pathetic statistic. But please, tell me more about Mercy's future prospects."

Wyatt's face contorts, his mouth. "Your management?" He sneers at me. "Your management, Savannah? With your whore of a mouth wrapped around that degenerate's cock in that biker club? Is that the family image you're managing?"

Holy shit, I'd forgotten about that leak. So many things happened since that day, it just... slipped my mind. I don't go online to gossip. I don't socialize anywhere. I don't belong to any groups and I don't covet and hoard hashtags like the professional influencers who view it as a job.

I post pictures, that's it.

So I don't really live in the same world as everyone else. Why should I? Even without the estate money, I have enough personal money for two lifetimes.

Legion was wrong about that. Thinking my money would run out in a year if we escaped and just gave into the urge to be 'regular people'.

My money will never run out. I have stacks of it everywhere. In the safe, buried down in the bedrock. In the barn. Buried in various spots on the property. And that's just my pocket money should anything happen with the legitimate stuff that's in the bank.

Colt and I started doing this when we were young. Pretendin' we were cowboys who robbed banks. It was a play thing. But then, as we got older, as the sums got real, we made a decision together that we'd stash half of what we got paid out in the trust each year.

Just in case.

I've always had plenty. My trust pays out two point three million every January like clockwork. Much more than his did. But he must've saved a lot over the last fifteen years since he came of age, because he didn't blink when he walked away from everything so he could keep his child bride and brand-new baby.

"That's enough, Wyatt," Cash says calmly.

I sigh, pulling myself back to the dumpster fire that is my family life.

"No," Wyatt says. "She thinks she's so fucking high and mighty. So much better than the rest of us. She was on her knees, between his legs, sucking his dick like she couldn't get enough. It was disgusting. You're disgusting, Savannah."

"That's *enough*," Cash repeats.

"Fuck off, Cash," Wyatt retorts. He's still looking at me. "You know why there hasn't been an uproar, Savannah? Do you have any idea why it disappeared so quickly? It was Marcus. He paid all those people—every person who posted it—five-thousand dollars to take it down and shut the fuck up. He paid for an army of bots to troll every corner of the internet searching for it, then threatened to sue anyone who didn't take it down."

He shoves back from the table, knocking over his orange juice. "So I don't wanna hear how you're the one polishing the Ashby image, Savannah. You're the trash we need to take out. And if it were up to me, I'd give you back to Marcus in a heartbeat. He paid enough for you. Might as well get his money's worth."

I freeze, the air punched from my lungs.

Wyatt storms out, slamming the door behind him.

Cash sighs, dabbing at the spilled juice with his napkin. "Ignore him. He's high. Doesn't know what he's saying."

But I can't ignore it. Wyatt's words burrow into my brain, unearthing something I'd deliberately buried—Marcus's claim that I was promised to him.

I hadn't let myself think about it since the kidnapping. Not with everything Legion went through after—the infection, the brand, nearly dying. But now the memory rises like bile in my throat.

"Your mother had been grooming you since childhood to be the perfect political wife."

"Our marriage was arranged before your birth."

I'd dismissed it as the ravings of a deranged man. But what if it wasn't? What if I really was sold off like one of our prize heifers?

"Cash," I say, my voice smaller now. "Did… was I… promised to Marcus in some way?"

He doesn't answer immediately, which is answer enough.

"It wasn't like that," he finally says, not meeting my eyes. "It was an arrangement. Beneficial to everyone. The Whites have connections we need."

I close my eyes, exhaling slowly. "How many times a day," I ask, opening my eyes, "does one have to be reminded that no one around them cares?"

Cash stares at me for a long moment, then stands, straightening his collar. "I have work to do." He hesitates at the doorway. "The auction. Tuesday. Be ready by nine."

And then he's gone, leaving me alone at the table with cooling coffee and congealed eggs.

This is what life without Legion feels like—present in body, gone in spirit. We will fuck, and we will do it regularly, but we will live separate lives. That's the current state—and maybe the future. A series of midnight meetings at the silo, brief moments of connection in a life otherwise spent apart.

I pull out my phone, scrolling through contacts until I find Colt's name. I've tried calling dozens of times, but it always goes straight to voicemail. I want to find him, to know he, and Destiny, and little Marigold are safe. But there's no trail. No charges on the family accounts. He's disappeared completely and his trust fund buried treasure was how he did it.

I don't really understand what's happening with Marigold, but I know Cash is stressed about it. What she means for the will and Eleanor's estate. A Kane by blood, but an Ashby by name. The lawyers are having a field day with it.

Nothing is final until I marry. "Properly." That was Eleanor's stipulation. The ultimate control from beyond the grave.

But I won't. Maybe ever.

Because the only man I'd marry is the one I'm not allowed to have.

I stare at my phone for a long time after Cash

leaves. The screen dims, then goes dark. I press the power button to light it up again. Marcus's contact sits there, untouched for weeks. The last message from him —sent while I was at the clubhouse with Legion— reads: *Call me. We can fix this.*

My thumb hovers over his name.

I don't want to call him. Every cell in my body rejects the idea. But if what Wyatt said is true—if Marcus paid to have that video scrubbed from the internet—then I owe him... *something*. Not gratitude. Never that. Not after what he did to me in that cabin.

But acknowledgment, at least.

The world, after all, works on favors.

Debts paid and collected.

That's the currency of the elite.

I walk to the window, phone still in hand. Outside, the ranch sprawls in every direction, forty-seven thousand acres of Ashby land. My land. The horses graze in the pasture, the cattle low in the distance. All mine. But only if I play by Eleanor's rules.

"Fuck," I whisper, pressing my forehead against the cool glass.

I press call before I can talk myself out of it.

He answers on the third ring. "Savannah." His voice is smooth, controlled. No hint of the man who tied me to a bed and force-fed me cherry pie. "I was beginning to think you'd never call."

"I need to know if it's true," I say, skipping any pretense of pleasantries.

"You'll have to be more specific."

"The video. Of me and Legion at the clubhouse. Wyatt says you paid to have it taken down."

There's a pause, and I can almost see him sitting in his study, adjusting his cufflinks, considering his response.

"Yes," he finally says. "I did."

I close my eyes, exhaling slowly. "Why?"

"Why do you think?" A hint of irritation creeps into his voice. "It wasn't exactly flattering footage, Savannah. You on your knees in a biker bar, surrounded by criminals, with a cock down your throat."

I swallow hard, remembering that night. How desperate I'd been to prove I belonged with Legion. How I let myself be claimed in front of everyone. The memory should shame me, but it doesn't. It feels like freedom—the one time I truly chose for myself.

"I didn't ask you to do that," I say.

"No, you were too busy playing outlaw's whore to consider the consequences." The words are harsh, but his tone remains even. Clinical. "Someone had to protect the Ashby name. And the White name, by extension."

"I'm not calling to thank you," I clarify, gripping the phone tighter. "But I want you to know I won't press charges for what you did to me at the cabin."

He laughs, the sound so unexpected it makes me flinch. "Charges, Savannah? On what grounds? That I took care of my fiancée when she was having a mental break? That I protected her from herself? Good luck with that narrative."

"You drugged me. Kept me tied to a bed."

"I sedated you under medical supervision when you became violent. I restrained you when necessary for your own safety." His voice drops lower. "Who do you think a judge would believe, Savannah? The senator's son with an impeccable record, or the heiress who's been fucking a convicted felon?"

The truth of his words lands like a slap. Power has never been about what's right—only about who has the leverage to make their version of events the official one.

"I didn't do it for you anyway," Marcus continues, his voice softening into something almost kind. Which, somehow makes it worse. "I did it for myself."

"What does that mean?"

"It means you're still going to be my wife, Savannah."

The room seems to tilt beneath me. "No. That's over."

"Is it?" Another soft laugh. "Nothing's changed. You can live your own life. You can fuck anyone you want— hell, you can suck your biker's dick all day and night as long as you don't get caught. But you *will* marry me, and you *will* stand by my side like a good little political wife when I tell you to."

Who the hell does he think he is? "I won't."

"You *will*. Because there's no getting out of it. It's for the best. A win-win for both families." His voice takes on that practiced political cadence he uses at fundraisers. "Expect to hear from my lawyer."

The call drops before I can respond.

I lower my phone slowly, staring at the ended call screen. My hand trembles slightly. I feel cold all over, despite the warm Montana sunshine streaming through the window.

Marcus thinks he's won. That I'll fall in line like I always have, smile for the cameras, play my part in his political ascension. Maybe he's right. Maybe there is no escape from the life Eleanor crafted for me.

But Eleanor never accounted for Legion Kane. For what happens when you spend your whole life performing, then finally taste what it means to be real.

I look down at my wrist, at the "PROPERTY OF DEMON" tattoo hidden beneath my watch. Legion may have walked away, but I'm still wearing his mark.

Still his, whether he wants me or not.

And tonight I'll show him just how much he's missing by pushing me away.

CHAPTER 4
LEGION

I enter the meeting hall at noon, muscles tight under my cut. The building we hold church in stands apart from the main clubhouse. Concrete block walls, a single metal door with a locking bar across it, and no windows.

No chance for prying eyes or listening ears.

The floor is stained concrete, bearing decades of spilled whiskey, blood, and promises. Overhead, fluorescent lights buzz like angry wasps, casting everyone in a sickly pallor.

At the front, a raised platform holds the long wooden table where Brick and the officers sit. Diesel nods at me. Not sure if that's an I-got-your-back nod or what, but I guess I'm gonna find out.

Behind them hangs our flag—skull wrapped in barbed wire rising from cracked earth—and the memorial wall with photos of brothers who died wearing the patch.

Sixty chairs face them, all arranged in rows. All

patched members are present, plus the so-called nomads who hang back, by the exit.

Brick's gavel cracks against the table. "Church is in session," he announces. "Lock it down."

Someone secures the door, turns the key, and drops it in the metal lockbox. Nobody comes in or out until Brick says so. Those are the rules.

"Brothers," Brick continues, looking around the room. "We've got blood on our floor and questions that need answering."

Chains spits on the ground. "Fuckin' right we do."

"Shut it," Roach snaps from beside Brick. "President's got the floor."

"First order of business," Brick says, tapping a folder in front of him. "We've got rats in the walls."

There is an intake of breath here. Before Diesel's confession, I probably would've mistaken it as surprise. But they're not surprised. They're resigned.

They don't all look at me—most of them have more control. But at least half a dozen do.

And again, before Diesel's confession, I'd take that as an accusation. Hell, it probably still is, in some way.

But that's not really why they're lookin' at me. They're lookin' at me because I'm the reason for this meeting.

It's not about me being the rat. It's about me being a hold out after this meeting's over.

"Three runs gone sideways in a month," Brick goes on. Continuing with the charade. "That's no coincidence, brothers. That's..." He pauses, lets the moment drag on. "That's incompetence."

Incompetence, huh?

Not a rat, then?

Not yet, at least. But it's set up that way.

Brick stares directly at me, his gaze cold as Montana winter. I remember when those eyes held something like pride. When he'd clap my shoulder after a successful run, call me "the future of this club."

Those days are gone. Ever since I brought Savannah here, something changed in him.

I thought it was about her family. Their influences. And maybe some of it is.

But that's not the real reason.

Then I thought it was the drama.

And that's definitely part of it too.

But only in a second-cousin kind of way.

Drama equals attention. Attention equals eyeballs.

Eyeballs Brick, and his little posse of Feds, don't need right now.

There is no "National Association of Outlaw Bikers". Not officially, anyway. But word travels, and drama this big, travels fast.

They need to balance this attention, and they need to do it quick.

And they're gonna use me to do it.

The only one that hasn't agreed to be a rat.

That's what Brick is lookin' for. He wants me to be a sellout, like everyone else.

And I get it, the brothers don't have much of a say if their prez goes rogue and cuts a deal. Either they have his back, and the protection he's negotiating, or they don't, and end up dead, or in prison, or worse.

The brand on my chest throbs, the scar tissue still angry and red. Brick holds that against me too—that I let it get infected. Like I did it on purpose. Like I wanted to end up at the Ashby ranch, recovering in a bed where every passing minute made me feel like an invalid.

His eyes are different now. Harder. Emptier. The eyes of a man who's made a decision about you before you've opened your mouth.

I've seen those eyes before. In Whitefall. Right before someone got shanked in the yard.

They didn't used to be this way—at least, not when he was looking at me.

But that's not really true, is it?

My mind flashes back to that first meeting with Brick—out in Makoshika with a shotgun for huntin' turkeys.

I don't know what you think you just saw, so I'm gonna tell you what you just saw to make sure we're clear. You saw a gun deal. You saw our hidey hole. You saw something you should not have. So you've got two choices, kid. One—I'm a liar and that's not what you saw at all. Or two—they find your body out here when the snow melts in spring.

Back then, I thought it was theater. A show to scare a kid straight. I spent years after that day trying to find my way into his world, believing that threat had just been part of the performance.

I was wrong.

The gun was real. The threat was real. And the look in his eyes now is the same one I saw that day in the brush. The look of a man deciding whether you live or die.

Only this time, there's no shrubs to hide in. No home to run back to. Just a president who looks at me like I'm already a ghost, and a bunch of men who don't seem to be my brothers anymore.

Brick leans forward, folding his hands on the table. "Demon Kane," he says, using my club name like it's already been stripped away. "Three jobs. Three failures. All on your watch."

The accusation hangs there. Sharp and poisonous.

"First run—you showed up thirty minutes late to the drop point, costin' us ten grand and a truck full of product. Said you got the time wrong."

I didn't. The instructions came from him directly. Ten p.m. at the old quarry. I was there at 9:45, watching headlights that never came because someone tipped off the buyers not to show.

"Second run—you took the north route when the orders said east through Makoshika. You led two vans straight into a patrol checkpoint."

That's a lie too. Brick pulled me aside before that run, grabbed my cut, and said, "North route. Through the badlands. Don't deviate."

"Third run—last night. You insisted on taking Butch instead of Hammer, even though the manifest clearly stated Hammer was assigned."

Bullshit. Pure bullshit. There was no manifest. Brick came to my room at 4 a.m., told me to take Butch and Dusty and make the exchange at the abandoned gas station off Route 12. I don't even know Hammer. He doesn't even live here. Couldn't pick him out in this room if I tried.

The room feels like it's shrinking. Every man watching, waiting. Some confused. Some already decided.

"You want to explain yourself, Demon?" Brick asks, but his tone says he doesn't expect an answer. Doesn't want one.

It's all bullshit.

And everyone in this fuckin' room knows it.

So why bother?

I say nothing.

He wants me to argue. He wants me to blame him so he has a reason to betray me, just like he did all the others.

But I don't make scenes. Never have.

And anyway, silence makes people uncomfortable. Makes them fill in the gaps with their own fears. Makes them wonder what you know, that they don't.

Six seconds pass. Ten. Fifteen.

Diesel shifts in his seat, arms crossed as his eyes dart between me and Brick. Ledger's hand inches toward his waistband. Roach picks at his teeth with a toothpick, but his eyes never leave me.

"Nothing to say for yourself?" Brick pushes. "No excuse? No defense?"

I just watch him. Let my eyes do the talking. Let him see that I know exactly what game he's playing.

The silence stretches longer. Some of the brothers look away, uncomfortable. Others lean forward, waiting for the explosion.

Brick's face hardens. "Alright then. The evidence speaks for itself." He looks around the table. "Given the pattern of failure, the club finds Demon Kane guilty of run interference, protocol violation, and operational security breach." He pronounces this like we took a vote. Like anyone besides him, had a say. "The penalty is a fine of twenty-five thousand dollars."

A low whistle from someone. They all know I don't have that kind of money.

Twenty-five thousand might as well be a million. Brick isn't imposing a fine. He's signing my death warrant. When you can't pay a club debt, you pay with blood instead.

"You have twenty-four hours," Brick says, his voice cold and final. "Funds delivered to this table by noon tomorrow or consequences will be enforced. Meeting adjourned."

The gavel comes down hard, like a headstone dropping into place.

Men rise from their seats, chairs scraping against concrete. The sound grates against my skull like a knife on bone. Twenty-five thousand dollars by tomorrow. Might as well ask for the moon on a fucking silver platter.

"You heard the president," Roach says to the room, voice pitched higher than usual. Nervous. "Meeting's over. Everyone out."

The room empties like someone pulled a drain plug. Men who stood beside me yesterday can't get away fast enough today. Some won't meet my eyes. Others stare too long, like they're memorizing my face for the last time.

Outside, movement in the doorway catches my eye. Brandy leans against the porch railing, arms crossed under her tits, lips curled in a smirk that makes my blood simmer. She's watching me like I'm already dead, like she's picking which pieces of my corpse she'll keep as souvenirs.

When our eyes meet, her smirk widens. No shame at all in what's happenin' here.

That's when I see it. The connection I've been missing.

Brandy isn't some rando hangaround. She's not some jailbait whore.

She's one of them.

A Fed.

Jesus Christ. How deep does this go if Brick's 'woman' is involved?

Was she sent here to spy on Brick? Or us? Or both?

Keep him in line?

What a fuckin' cuck. If she's here to keep Brick in line… I'm sorry. I'm done. How could I respect a man who will not only put our club at risk for a deal, but let himself be 'handled' by a chick who doesn't even look old enough to drink?

I got nothing left for that man.

A stupid girl.

It's an insult.

A big 'ol fuck-you from the Feds.

And he let them do it.

Not that I was gonna cut Brick any slack about this shit—a rat, is a rat, is a rat. Maybe, before I did my time, I'd have listened to his argument.

It'll keep us all out of prison.

They're gonna pay us.

Etc. Etc. Etc.

But after Whitefall, fuck that. Hell, no. No fuckin' way.

Rats are the lowest scum of the earth.

And I'm in a club with forty-seven of them.

Diesel appears at my side, matching my pace as I head toward the Dyna. His massive frame blocks the sun, casting me in shadow.

"This isn't what you think," he says, voice pitched high enough for me to understand that this is his assigned role in the charade we're playin'. "I need to tell you something, Legion…"

I sigh, blowin' out a breath. "OK." I play my part too, because I know every set of eyes is on me now. Including Brick's. All the Feds.

I am the weak link and they need me to turn or whatever they've set up here, it all goes to shit.

"He'll wave the fine. He just… wants you on board, ya know?"

I stop walking because I've reached my bike. I look Diesel in the eyes. I want to hate him right now. I want to cuss him out and call him a traitor.

"Patched in," I say. "What a fuckin' joke."

"I got you," he says. Sighin' a bit. "I felt the same way."

"Until?" I look behind me, watching Brick watch me. All the Feds are laughin' and jokin'. Like splittin' up brotherhoods is just something they do on Tuesdays.

"Until they gave me no choice."

I look back at Diesel. "Is that what this is? They're gonna kill me if I don't pay up?"

"No. Brick… he doesn't want that to happen, Legion. He gave you the fine knowing you can't pay so you'd—"

"Agree to be the rat with him? With you? With all of you?"

"Look," Diesel says. "I don't like it any more than you do. Do I wanna be a rat? Fuck, no. But do I want Mama Jo to go to prison for shit I did? Another 'fuck no'."

"Is that what they're threatening, then? The families?" I picture Ratchet and June. Their little ranch. Six kids, the dog, all of it at risk.

If I had that, I guess I'd turn too.

But I don't have that.

I got nothin'.

"Let me ask you somethin', Diesel. And I want the truth now." I look him in the eyes. "If I say no, you still got my back? Or was that nothin' but words to you?"

He lets out a long breath, lookin' over his shoulder at Brick. When he looks back at me, his words are low again. Meant only for me. "I got you."

I press my lips together and nod. "OK. Good to know." The sun beats down on my neck as I swing my leg over the seat. The engine roars to life beneath me, the familiar vibration traveling up my spine.

As I roll away from the garage, I scan the compound one last time.

I ride away from the clubhouse with nowhere to go and twenty-four hours to live.

Because I won't ever be the rat.

I'm never gonna be the rat.

I'd rather die.

And if I'm gonna die, then I got business to take care of.

Almost two hours later, Rimrock Academy appears over the ridge like something from another planet. All perfect sandstone buildings and manicured lawns. Green in a state that's mostly dust and dirt. The kind of place where the grass gets watered twice a day, no matter how much it doesn't rain.

I slow the bike as I approach the gate, suddenly aware of how I must look. Three-day stubble. Leather cut with the Badlands patch. Blood still under my fingernails from Butch, even after washing my hands.

The kind of man they build places like this to keep out.

The guard booth is manned by a guy in a pressed uniform who straightens when he sees me coming. His hand drifts toward something under the counter. Not exactly subtle.

"Help you?" he asks, eyes flicking from my face to my cut to my bike and back again. The bike idles so loud, I can barely hear him.

"I'm here to see my sister. Mercy Kane." My voice is loud and rough. "She's a student."

The guard's expression doesn't change. "You're not on the approved visitor list, sir."

"I'm her brother. Her legal guardian." The lie comes easy. I was her guardian, before Cash took her.

"I'll need to see some ID."

I reach slowly for my wallet, careful to telegraph every movement. The last thing I need is to get shot by some trigger-happy rent-a-cop. My license is new, at least. Savannah pulled in some favors while I was recovering and got it renewed in the mail. Something that didn't impress me much when she handed it over, but makes me feel the loss of her even more, here in the moment.

He takes it, studies it like it might be fake, then picks up a phone. The conversation happens without me. A low voice I can't quite make out. But he never takes his eyes off me.

The minutes stretch. One. Five. Eight. Ten. The sun beats down on my shoulders, and sweat trickles down my spine.

I keep cool. Waitin' it out.

There's no way I'm leaving here without seeing Mercy, and these people have to know that.

How can they cut their losses when Legion Kane shows up at the gate?

Let him in.

Finally, he hangs up and points down the drive. "Go ahead. Park at the main building and check in at the office." He hands back my license. "Visitor pass will be waiting."

"Thanks," I say.

The gates open and I ride on.

The road curves through campus, past buildings that look more like museums than classrooms. Kids in uniforms stop to stare as I pass. Their whispers follow me like a wake. The bike is too loud here, too dirty, too real among all this polish and pretend.

I find the main building easy enough. It's the biggest one, with stone columns and a clock tower. The kind of place that screams money with every brick. I park the Dyna near the entrance, swing my leg over, and stand for a moment, rolling my shoulders.

Every eye is on me. Students in their pressed uniforms. Teachers clutching books to their chests. A groundskeeper who's stopped his zero-turn mower to watch. I'm a wolf that's wandered into the sheep pen, and everyone knows it.

I give them all a general salute, and make my way inside where the air conditioning hits me like a wall. The lobby is all polished wood and glass cases full of trophies. A woman at the front desk looks up as I approach, her smile professional but wary.

"Legion Kane," I say before she can ask. "Here to see Mercy Kane. I was told there'd be a visitor pass."

"Yes, Mr. Kane." She slides a plastic badge across the counter. "We've notified Mercy's teacher. She should be here shortly."

I clip the badge to my cut, feeling ridiculous. Like putting a name tag on a gun.

But clearly, these people are trying their best to make me happy so…

Then she's here. Mercy's quick footsteps pound on the marble floor, running despite whatever rules they have against it. Her face is flushed, eyes wide with fear.

"Legion!" She skids to a stop in front of me, searching my face. "What's wrong? Is it Savannah? Is someone hurt?"

Fuck. It didn't even occur to me that comin' here would send a signal like that. "Nothing's wrong, Merce. Everyone's fine."

Her breathing is still too fast. "But you're here. In the middle of the day."

"Just wanted to see you, that's all." I try for a smile, but the lie feels wrong on my face. "I miss you.

Thought maybe we could take a walk. If that's allowed."

Mercy's eyes narrow slightly. She's always been too good at reading me. "You never just visit."

"First time for everything."

A woman appears behind Mercy, clipboard in hand. "Mr. Kane, I'm Ms. Holbrook, Mercy's advisor. Mercy can have thirty minutes for her visit, but she'll need to return for her next class."

I nod. "Understood."

"There's a walking path around the quad," she adds, gesturing toward the door. "Please stay on campus grounds."

"Yes, ma'am," I say, automatically.

She's got the nerve to blush before quickly turning and walking away.

Outside, Mercy guides me toward a stone path that circles a grassy area. She's different already. Stands straighter. Walks with purpose. Her uniform is pristine.

"You look good, Mercy." I mean it. "School treating you right?"

She nods, some of the tension leaving her shoulders. "It's pretty fun. I never thought I'd say that about school, but I like it. The food's really good. And I have my own room!"

"That so?"

"Yes, a dorm room. I share it with four other girls, but it's still mine. And I'm in the science club. We're gonna build rockets this semester!" Her voice picks up speed, excitement breaking through. "And I've made a horse friend. Her name's Emma. We ride on Mondays and Wednesdays."

I listen as she rattles off more details—teachers' names, books she's reading, the fact that they get ice cream on Fridays. All the little things that make up an exceptional childhood. Things I never could have given her.

"So you're happy here?" I ask, when she pauses for breath.

Mercy looks up at me, suddenly serious. "Are you okay, Legion? You look tired."

"I'm fine." This lie comes easier. "Just been working a lot."

"At the club?"

I nod, not trusting my voice.

"Savannah says you can visit with me on the weekends at the estate. If you want." Her eyes search mine. "Do you want to?"

What I want is to grab her and run. Take her far away from Cash, and Brick, and everyone else who's trying to use us. But that's not what she needs.

"I want you to be happy, Mercy. That's all I've ever wanted."

She's quiet for a moment, thinking. "I am. Happy, I mean. It's weird, but...I like it here."

Somethin' inside me eases at her words. At least I've done one thing right.

"Then this is where you should be."

We walk the path twice, Mercy pointing out buildings and telling me stories about her classes. Normal things. Safe things. I listen, and nod, and try to memorize every detail of her face.

When Ms. Holbrook appears at the edge of the quad, I know our time is up.

"Gotta go," Mercy says, glancing at her advisor. "Will you be there on Saturday, then? At home?"

Home. Which isn't the trailer. It's the Ashby Ranch. "I'll try." Another lie. I don't know where I'll be on Saturday. Don't know if I'll be anywhere at all.

She hugs me quickly, fiercely, then pulls back. "Tell Savannah I said hi."

"I will."

I watch her run back to Ms. Holbrook, back to her new life. She turns once to wave, and I raise my hand in response.

The walk back to the bike is longer somehow. More eyes on me. More whispers. I don't care. All that matters is that Mercy is safe. Happy. Better off without me.

I swing my leg over the Dyna and fire it up.

The clock in my head is tickin'.

Hours slipping away, bringing me closer to midnight.

Closer to Savannah.

Closer to whatever end Brick has planned for me, too.

CHAPTER 5
SAVANNAH

Eleven twenty-five.

I check my watch again, though I know exactly what time it is. I've been watching the minutes tick by since dinner ended, since Cash finally retreated to his study, since I locked my bedroom door and changed.

Five minutes. That's all that's left before I need to be gone.

Marcus's voice still echoes in my head. His certainty. His casual ownership. The way he said, "We both know how this ends, Savannah," like my life was already written and I just hadn't accepted the final chapter yet.

Fuck him.

I smooth down the white summer dress—shorter than I'd normally wear around the ranch, thin enough to show shadows of what's underneath. It's not about looking pretty. It's about access. Legion's hands finding my skin as quickly as possible. The dress coming off easily.

It's always about sex with him. Especially now. We

don't talk anymore—not really. Not since he left without saying goodbye. Not since I slapped him and he pushed me against the wall, both of us panting with rage that turned into something else entirely.

I don't care. I'll take Legion Kane any way I can get him. I just need him inside me. Need to feel something that isn't this crushing weight of loss and expectations.

I open my bedroom door, listening for any movement in the house. Nothing. Cash sleeps like the dead after his nightly bourbon. Wyatt's probably passed out in some corner. The staff all retire to their quarters by ten.

But this is just habit. There's no sneaking required. Not anymore.

Marcus literally gave me permission to sneak out and fuck Legion.

Not that I need it.

The night air hits my skin as I step outside, still warm from the day's heat. I don't bother with the side entrance to the barn—I use the main doors, flipping on lights as I go. Cassia looks up from her stall, ears pricked forward.

"Hey girl," I murmur, grabbing her bridle. "Time for our midnight ride."

I don't bother with a saddle, never do when I'm on my way to the silo. Just lead her over to the mounting platform and get on.

I guide her toward the back pasture, making no attempt to hide in the shadows. The moon is nearly full tonight, lighting up the grass, making it silver. I don't jump her over the fence tonight. Just open the gate, walk her through to freedom, and kick it closed with my toe after we're out.

Once we're on the grass, I give Cassia her freedom too. She breaks into a slow canter, knowing the way as well as I do by now. The path to the silo is worn into my memory, into her muscles. We've made this journey so many times.

Twenty minutes later, the old grain silo appears on the horizon, a dark cylinder against the star-filled sky. I slow Cassia to a walk as we approach, giving her time to cool down. No Legion yet. His bike isn't here.

I dismount, my dress riding up as I slide down, then leave Cassia to graze, her reins fastened into the chinstrap of her bridle. She won't wander far.

Then I pace around the silo entrance, checking my watch again and again as the seconds tick towards midnight.

My body responds to the distinctive growl of his bike cutting through the quiet night. Instantly, heat is pooling between my legs. I stand still, watching as his headlight bounces over the uneven ground, growing brighter as he approaches.

Legion kills the engine but leaves the headlight on, illuminating me in its beam. I can see him clearly— leather cut over bare chest, jeans worn in all the right places, boots kicking up dust as he dismounts. He walks toward me slowly, deliberately, eyes never leaving mine. I don't move. Won't give him the satisfaction of seeing me eager, even though my heart is poundin' so hard I can feel it in my throat.

When he reaches me, he doesn't speak. Doesn't

smile. Just grabs my face with both hands and crashes his mouth against mine.

Everything ignites. My hands are in his hair, pulling him closer. His are already sliding up my thighs, finding the edge of my underwear. We stumble backward until my shoulders hit the metal wall of the silo.

"No talking," he growls against my mouth, as if I was about to start a conversation.

I bite his lower lip in response, hard enough to make him hiss. "Shut up and fuck me."

His hands are everywhere at once—ripping my underwear down my legs, shoving my dress up around my waist, squeezing my breasts through the thin fabric. I'm fumbling with his belt, desperate to feel him. The zipper gives way under my fingers and I push his jeans down just enough to free him.

His cock is already hard, hot and heavy in my hand. I stroke him roughly, watching his eyes darken.

"Get on your knees," he commands, voice low and dangerous.

I sink down in front of him, the cool grit of the ground biting into my bare knees. He reaches down, pulling on the hem of my dress. Yanking it over my head and tossing it aside.

I look up at him through my lashes, meeting his gaze. His eyes are the same. Haven't changed since we were teenagers sneaking out past midnight. Without breaking that connection, I take him in my mouth, welcoming his thick length between my lips. My tongue traces the underside of his shaft, teasing the sensitive spot just below the head. The weight of him fills my mouth completely—heavy with need, pulsing with a hunger that matches my own desperate craving.

I work him deeper, letting my lips stretch around his girth, savoring the way his breath catches when I swallow around him.

His fingers curl tighter into my hair. "That's it," he groans. "Show me how much you missed this cock."

The rawness in his words sends electricity down my spine, pooling between my thighs where I'm already soaked and aching. I take him deeper, proving with actions what we both already know—that I crave this lust like a drug.

The taste of him is intoxicating, familiar yet somehow new, like revisiting a favorite memory only to find it's even more powerful than you remembered. I worship him with my mouth, communicating everything I can't say with words. Moaning and taking him deeper, using my tongue the way I know drives him crazy.

His grip tightens painfully in my hair. "Enough," he says. Pushing me off him and hauling me to my feet. "My turn."

He spins me around, bending me forward until my hands brace against the silo wall. My ass is up, exposing me completely to the night air. I hear him drop to his knees behind me, and then his mouth is on me, his teeth biting into the flesh of my hips as he pushes a finger up against my asshole.

The unexpected pressure makes me gasp and arch my back.

He's never taken me there before, never even hinted

at it during our countless rendezvous in this rusted metal sanctuary.

But I won't say no if he wants to tonight.

The thought of him claiming this final, forbidden territory sends a shiver of both fear and anticipation through my body. I can't say no to him—not for anything sexual. Every boundary I've ever established crumbles to dust when Legion touches me like this.

I want him to claim me in every way possible, to mark me as his in ways that will linger long after I've returned to my picture-perfect life at the ranch.

I cry out, shamelessly pushing back against his face when he begins to lick me. His hands grip my ass cheeks, holding me open as he devours me. His tongue circles my clit relentlessly before dipping inside me, tasting how wet I am for him.

"Legion," I gasp, already close to the edge. "Please—"

He pulls away abruptly, leaving me trembling and desperate. "Not yet."

Standing up, he positions himself behind me, the head of his cock teasing my entrance. I try to push back, to take him inside, but his hand on my hip holds me still.

"Beg for it," he demands.

"Fuck you," I spit back, though we both know I'll give in. I always do.

His palm connects with my ass in a sharp slap that makes me yelp. His command darker now. "I said, beg for it."

"Please," I whisper, my voice breaking with need as I

swallow what's left of my pride. "Please fuck me, Legion. I need you inside me."

Before the words are even out of my mouth, he does. He slams his cock into my pussy with such force, my face is pushed against the silo.

Then he leans closer, his breath hot against my ear, his chest pressing against my back. "More. Talk to me, Savannah. Tell me exactly what you want. Every dirty thought that's been haunting you since I went away. Every shameful fantasy you touched yourself to while I was locked in that cell. Every filthy detail you've been saving for this moment right here."

"I want you to fuck me so hard I can't walk straight tomorrow," I breathe, my voice shaking. "I want to feel you for days. Want bruises on my hips from your fingers. Want to be sore every time I sit down at breakfast with Cash and remember exactly how you wrecked me."

"This what you want?" he grunts, fingers digging into my hips hard enough to bruise. "This what you left your fancy house for? To get fucked by trailer trash?"

"Yes," I moan, pushing back to meet each thrust. "God, yes."

He reaches around, fingers finding my clit, circling it in time with his thrusts. "You like being my whore, don't you? Rich girl slumming it with a criminal."

The words should offend me, but they only make me hotter. This is what we are now—all the hurt and anger channeled into something physical, something we can control.

"I'm yours," I pant, feeling my orgasm building. "Only yours."

He slows suddenly, his thrusts becoming shallow, teasing. "Show me. Touch yourself."

I reach between my legs, my fingers finding their way to join his on my clit, our touch intertwining in a desperate, intimate dance. The dual sensation sends electric currents racing through my body, overwhelming every sense until I'm trembling against him, gasping for air. My lungs burn with each shallow breath as the pressure builds within me, coiling tighter and tighter like a spring about to snap. I'm balanced on the knife's edge of release, so achingly close that coherent thought dissolves into pure, primal need, leaving me dizzy and desperate in the darkness of our sacred, rusted cathedral.

His cock presses harder against my entrance, just barely breaching me. Not enough. Never enough.

"Keep going," he growls.

"I touched myself every night you were gone," I confess, the words spilling out in a rush now that I've started. "In my bed at the mansion, in the shower, in my car parked on the side of the road when I couldn't wait anymore. I'd think about your hands on me, your mouth, the way you look at me like I'm the only thing in the world that matters, even though we both know that's a lie."

He spits on my asshole, rubbing it around with the tip of his cock. "What else?" His voice is rough, strained with his own need as he presses the head of his dick against my tight resistance.

"I imagined this," I admit, shame and arousal mixing into something toxic and addictive. "You bending me over, taking what you want without asking. Using me like I'm nothing but a hole for you to fuck whenever you get bored with your club brothers. Making me beg for your cock in my ass like some desperate whore who can't live without it."

"Because you can't," he says, and it's not a question.

"No," I whisper, finally admitting the truth we've both been dancing around. "I can't. I need you inside me, Legion. Any way you want to take me, I'm yours. I need you to fuck me until I forget my own name, forget Marcus, and Cash, and every single obligation waiting for me back at that house. I need you to make me feel like I'm yours, even if it's only for tonight. Even if you're going to leave me again tomorrow, and not answer my texts, and pretend I don't exist until the next time you're hard and desperate."

The words hang in the air between us, too honest, too raw. This is what he does to me—strips away every layer of polish and performance until there's nothing left but the desperate girl underneath who would do anything, say anything, to keep him.

"I fantasized about you fucking me in front of the whole club again," I continue, giving him everything now because what's left to protect? "Not just showing them I'm yours, but letting them watch while you use me. While you prove that the Ashby princess is really just your personal fuck toy. I touched myself thinking about you sharing me with—"

"No." The word comes out sharp, possessive. His cock slams into me without warning, filling me completely in one brutal thrust that tears a scream from my throat.

"You're mine," he snarls against my ear, his hips already setting a punishing rhythm. "Only mine. Say it."

"Yours," I gasp, my hands scrabbling against the metal wall for purchase as he fucks into me mercilessly. "Only yours, always yours—"

"Louder."

"I'M YOURS!" I scream into the Montana night, not caring who might hear, not caring about anything except the feeling of him inside me, claiming me, making good on every promise his body has ever made to mine.

His hand snakes around to rub my clit while he pounds into me from behind, and I'm already so close, have been on the edge since his mouth first touched me. The dual sensations—his cock stretching me open—tight and painful, but also a rush of pleasure I've never experienced before. His fingers work my clit, his teeth biting down on my hip—all of this together pushes me over into oblivion.

I come with a broken sob, my whole body convulsing around him. But he doesn't stop, doesn't slow down, just keeps fucking me through it until I'm trembling, and oversensitive, and still somehow desperate for more.

"Again," he demands, his fingers still circling my clit even though I'm whimpering from the intensity. "Come again, Savannah. Show me how much you need this cock."

"I can't—too much—Legion, please—"

"You can." His free hand tangles in my hair, pulling my head back so he can bite down on my neck. "You will. Because you're mine and I own this ass and every orgasm inside you. Now *fucking come for me.*"

The pain mixed with pleasure as he pounds me, the command in his voice, his fingers, pressing against my clit, the feeling of being completely at his mercy—it all combines into another wave that crashes over me.

I come again, harder this time, my legs shaking and trembling until they actually give out. Only his arm around my waist keeps me upright as he continues to thrust into my spasming body.

"That's it," he groans, his rhythm finally faltering. "Fuck, Savannah—"

He buries himself deep one last time and, then he pulls out. He spins me around, aims his cock at my face, and comes all over my mouth.

I lick it up like nothing has ever taste so good.

Then he drops to his knees beside me, hands on my face, wiping his come of my lips, and kisses me. He kisses me hard. Almost angry. "I love you," he says. "I love you so fucking much, Savannah. You know that, right? You know that. You have to know that. Whatever we do here, the sex. The dirty talk. That's all it is, just talk. You're not a fuck toy. You're not a whore. You're…"

But he stops.

Because I'm looking at him.

And I'm suddenly thinking… "What's happening here?"

"What do you mean?"

He knows what I mean. This sex. Oh, it was good. I want to keep going. I want him to fuck me all night long.

But it's… wrong. Not the anal. Not what we did.

Why we're doing it.

He's never wanted to take me in the ass before. Why tonight?

"What happened?" I ask him.

"What are you talking about?"

"Something happened. I liked the sex, Legion. But this was…"

"Incredible," he smiles.

"Yeah, but—"

"You want it again?"

"Stop changing the subject. What's going on?"

CHAPTER 6
LEGION

I pull Savannah close, guilt washing through me like flood water. My hands shake as I wrap them around her body, pressing her against my chest where she can feel my heart hammering.

Why did I take her like that? Like I was trying to fuck my way through to something on the other side. Like this might be the last time.

Like I'm already dead or disappeared.

"What's wrong?" she asks again, softer now. Her palm presses against my chest, right over the ruined brand. "Legion, talk to me."

I can't. So I deflect.

"You remember that summer I got the dirt bike?"

She goes still in my arms. "What?"

"The dirt bike. When I was fifteen. You were thirteen."

"Well... yes. Of course I remember."

"You had that big fancy thoroughbred your mother

bought you. You'd ride her out to Makoshika, and I'd take the bike. Meetin' up at the trailheads."

Savannah pulls back enough to look at my face. Her eyes search mine, trying to figure out what the hell I'm doing, bringing up ancient history while her ass is still burning from what I just did to her.

"You took me to see the dinosaur fossils," she says slowly. "It was a hundred degrees. I got so sunburned my shoulders blistered."

"I gave you my shirt."

"You did." Her hand moves from my chest to my face, thumb brushing my cheekbone. "You wrapped it around my shoulders and made me wear your stupid baseball cap even though it was way too big for me."

I remember the way she looked—this tiny blonde thing drowning in my clothes, her nose pink from the sun. We hiked three miles into the badlands to see some formation she'd read about in a library book. Fossil beds, or some shit. I didn't care about dinosaurs. I cared about the way her eyes lit up when she talked about things that mattered to her.

"Best summer of my life," I tell her. It comes out rough.

"Mine too." She traces the line of my jaw. "Before everything got complicated."

Before I joined the club. Before she left for boarding school. Before Eleanor started paying me to sit in her studio while she photographed me like I was art instead of a person. Before prison, before Marcus, before I learned how to break things, instead of protect them.

"I'm sorry," I say, and I mean it for more than just tonight. For all of it. For being too rough just now, for fucking her ass like I was trying to punish something—her, me, the world. "I shouldn't have—"

"Don't." She presses her fingers to my lips. "Don't apologize for that. I wanted it. You didn't hurt me. I'm not made of glass, Legion."

But she is. She's made of light, and air, and everything good I've ever touched, and I keep putting my filthy hands on her anyway.

"You're everything clean," I tell her. My voice cracks on the words. "Everything good. And I just keep—"

"Stop." She kisses me before I can finish the thought. Slow and deep, her mouth soft against mine. When she pulls back, her eyes are wet. "I'm not clean. I'm not good. I'm just... yours. That's all I've ever been."

I kiss her again because I can't fucking help myself. Pour everything I can't say into it—the goodbye I won't speak out loud, the thank you that doesn't go far enough, the love that's going to outlive both of us, and probably burn the world down in the process.

When we break apart, I rest my forehead against hers.

"Thank you," I whisper. "For taking care of me when I was dying. For loving Mercy. For—"

"You don't need to thank me for loving you." Her voice is fierce. "That's not... it's not something you earn or pay back. It just is."

I think about that. About how people like me don't get loved. We get used. We get feared. We get forgotten in prison cells and buried in unmarked graves when the club decides we're more valuable dead ,than breathing.

Except by her.

She's loved me since she was twelve years old and I

was fourteen and neither of us knew what the fuck love even meant.

"You had that pink helmet," I say, because I need to stay in the memory a little longer. Need to live there instead of here. "With the flowers on it."

Savannah laughs, the sound breaking through the heavy air between us. "Oh my god, I forgot about that helmet."

"It was hideous."

"It was *adorable*."

"It was pink."

"I was thirteen!" She swats my chest, and for a second she looks like that girl again—the one who'd show up at the silo with dirt on her jeans and wildflowers in her hair. "And you said it made me look like a wildflower fairy."

I did say that. Meant it too.

"You'd put it on," I continue, "and climb on the back of my bike, and we'd just... ride. For hours. Through all those backroads. The trails. Places nobody else went."

"I'd hold on to you so tight." Her fingers trace patterns on my chest, following the lines of ink and scar tissue. "Like if I let go, you'd disappear."

Maybe she knew something I didn't.

"Even back then," I tell her, "I'd look at you and think... that's my girl. Nobody else knew it. But I did."

"I was," she confirms. Her eyes find mine. "I still am."

I want to believe that. Want to live in the world where thirteen-year-old Savannah and fifteen-year-old Legion could just keep riding forever through the badlands. Immortal, and free, and too stupid to know what the future would cost.

"Best summer of my life," I say again. "Nothing's been that clean since."

She's quiet for a long moment. Then… "We could go back."

"What?"

"Not literally. But we could… try. To be those kids again. The ones who didn't know how to ruin things yet."

I look at her—this woman who left Marcus's engagement party to fuck me in a silo, who got my name tattooed on her wrist after I took the fall for a crime I didn't commit, who stood in a room full of outlaws and let me claim her in front of everyone because she chose this life over everything else.

And I think about how in twenty-four hours, I might be dead, or disappeared, or worse.

How Brick's twenty-five-thousand-dollar fine is really just a death sentence with paperwork.

How Savannah deserves better than watching me bleed out in some Montana ditch because I wouldn't become a rat.

"Yeah," I lie. "Maybe we could."

She smiles. Believes me. Curls against my chest like she's got all the time in the world to figure it out.

And I hold her there in the silo where we first learned what wanting meant, letting myself pretend—just for a few more minutes—that we're still those kids racing across the badlands.

That summer could last forever.

That neither of us knows how this story ends.

I make myself a promise in the silence that follows.

Whatever's happening at the club—the Feds, Brick's betrayal, the twenty-five grand I don't have, the blood I'll probably pay in instead—none of it touches her.

Not Savannah.

Not the girl who rode bareback through the badlands with flowers in her hair.

If that's the only gift I ever give her, it'll be worth it. Keeping her away from that life. From what I've become. From the slow death the club deals, to everyone who stays too long.

She deserves better than watching me choose between becoming a rat or bleeding out in some ditch.

She deserves the life she's building at the ranch. The one where Mercy thrives at Rimrock Academy, and wears pink riding helmets, and doesn't know what a prospect does to earn his patch.

I want a do-over.

Want to lay Savannah down gentle and worship every inch of her skin like she's something sacred, instead of something I use. Want to erase the last hour —the roughness, the degradation, the way I made her beg and called her mine while treating her like property.

But I can't.

What's done is done. And trying to fix it now just feels performative. Like I'm playing the part of the man she wants me to be instead of showing her the truth.

This is who I am.

Not the gentle lover who whispers pretty things.

I'm the crude animal that lives in the dark. The one

who fucks rough, and leaves marks, and can't touch anything clean without destroying it.

So I don't try to pretty it up.

I help Savannah to her feet, steadying her when she wobbles. Hand over her white dress—now wrinkled and stained. Watch her pull it over her head, the fabric settling over skin that's already bruising where I gripped too hard.

She doesn't complain. Doesn't ask me to be softer next time.

Just pulls her panties up her legs, smooths the dress down, and looks at me with those blue eyes that see too much.

I tuck myself back into my jeans. Button. Zip. Pull my shirt over my head and shrug into my cut—the leather settling across my shoulders like the weight it is.

This is how I'll leave it.

Ugly, but true.

No apologies. No promises I can't keep. No fairy tale ending where the outlaw becomes the prince and the princess slums it in a trailer.

Just this: her in a white dress. Me in black leather. The space between us filled with everything we can't say.

"Come on," I tell her. Keeping my voice even. "I'll walk you back."

Savannah doesn't argue. Just takes my offered hand —her fingers small and pale against my scarred knuckles—and lets me lead her over to her horse.

Cassia's waiting where Savannah left her, reins trailing in the dirt, looking bored.

The mare huffs when she sees us. Probably judges me for what I just did to her rider.

I cup my hands for Savannah's bare foot—why does she always come barefoot? Then I give her a leg up into the saddle.

She settles onto Cassia's bare back, legs dangling, white dress riding up her thighs, looking down at me with an expression I can't read.

"Legion—"

"I'll see you," I interrupt. Because I can't hear whatever she's about to say. Can't stand here and pretend I deserve the concern in her voice or the love she keeps offering like it's free.

I turn to go, but words split the night open, stopping me.

"One word between us splits the very sky," she says quietly. "They come for us but still we strive to try."

The words freeze me mid-step.

My poem. The one I wrote when I was sixteen, still stupid enough to believe words could mean something permanent.

"To make a place where love can truly grow," Savannah continues, her voice steady. "To Hell with those above and those below."

I turn back slowly. Stare up at her sitting on that horse like some kind of vision in white. The moonlight catches her hair, turning it silver-gold.

"How—" My voice cracks. I clear my throat. Try again. "How do you remember that?"

She doesn't smile. Just looks down at me with those eyes that've been haunting me since I was fourteen years old.

Something twists in my chest. Something that feels like the brand—wrong, infected, eating me from the inside out.

She shifts on Cassia's back. Gathers the reins in one hand while the other rests against her thigh, fingers spread over the pale fabric.

"You wrote me a promise," she says. "Now I'll write you one."

I wait. Don't move. Don't breathe.

Savannah lifts her chin. Her voice comes clear and strong:

"Through fire and blood we walk the path alone,

Two souls condemned who carved this world from stone.

Let them come with judgment, sword, and chain—

We'll build our kingdom from the ash and pain."

Somethin' inside me cracks. Nah, it rips me the fuck open. Raw and bleeding. And she's not even done yet. She keeps going…

"No grace above will break what hell has made,

No fear below will stop this vow we've laid.

When all is lost and even angels fall—

You'll still be mine. I'll still be yours. Through all."

I stand there like a statue while her words echo.

Through fire and blood we walk the path alone…

Can't move. Can't speak. Can't do anything but watch her sit on that horse like some kind of warrior queen who just declared war on heaven and hell both.

My throat's closin' up. Eyes burning. Chest so tight, I might crack a rib just breathing.

Two souls condemned who carved this world from stone…

She wrote me a fucking poem.

Memorized mine. Gave me hers. Like we're trading vows in some cathedral made of blood and barbed wire.

I want to say somethin'. Anything. Want to tell her—

But the words won't come.

They never do when it matters.

Savannah doesn't wait for them anyway. She turns Cassia with a gentle press of her knee, the mare wheeling smooth as silk, and they disappear into the dark. No goodbye. No looking back over her shoulder.

Just gone.

Like she makes decisions and lives with them. No second-guessing. No begging me to chase her or promise her things I can't deliver. She said her piece. Laid down her vow. And now she's riding home because that's what you do—you make your choice, then you fucking stand on it.

I could learn something from that. From the resilience of Savannah Ashby. The girl who got drugged and tied to a bed, then came back swingin'.

Who got her videos leaked to the internet, then showed up at my side anyway.

Who watches me leave over and over, but never stops opening the door when I come back.

She's stronger than anyone gives her credit for. Stronger than me, maybe.

I light a cigarette with shaking hands. Take a drag, inhaling my own regrets. My bike's waiting where I left it. Matte black that sucks up the moonlight instead of reflecting it. I swing my leg over. Fire it up. Let the rumble vibrate through my bones like a second heartbeat.

Then I ride.

Back toward the compound. Back toward Brick and his Feds and the twenty-five grand I don't have. Back toward the hell I built with my own two hands.

The road unspools beneath me. Empty. Dark. Just me and the wind and the ghosts I carry.

I try to remember her poem. All of it. The way she did with mine. *Let them come with judgment, sword, and chain—*

But the words are already slipping. Fragmenting. I catch pieces but lose the whole.

We'll build our kingdom from the ash and pain. That part I remember. Because it sounds like something I'd say if I knew how to make words beautiful instead of blunt.

When all is lost and even angels fall—

The highway blurs. I blink hard. Blame the wind.

You'll still be mine. I'll still be yours. Through all.

Through all.

She means it too. I can tell. Savannah Ashby doesn't make idle promises or perform love for the cameras anymore. She burned that version of herself when she got my name tattooed on her wrist.

She's mine. I'm hers. Through whatever comes.

The thought should comfort me. Instead, it just makes everything worse. Because in twenty-four hours, I might be dead. Or disappeared. Or broken in ways that don't heal.

And she'll still be there. Still waiting. Still believing in the poem she wrote like it's scripture.

The rage hits me in the middle of the midnight nowhere. Slammin' into my chest like a fist.

Three years.

I did three fuckin' years for Brick Ransom.

The memory rises sharp and bitter. Vehicle registered in my name. Product found during a traffic stop I wasn't even part of. Burner phone in the glove box with my fingerprints because Brick asked me to grab it that morning.

Feds offered deals. Tried to flip me six different ways.

I said nothing.

Signed the plea agreement. Took the conviction. Went to Whitefall and kept my mouth shut for thirty-six months while the brothers on the outside got to ride free.

Because that's what you do. You take the fall. You protect the club. You come home with your patch and your head high because loyalty means something.

Except, it doesn't.

Not anymore.

Brick sold out anyway.

Let the Feds infiltrate. Let them wear our colors, and sit at our table, and vote on our business like they're real brothers instead of fucking rats with badges.

And now he wants *me* to roll over too?

The speedometer climbs. Eighty. Ninety. The bike screams beneath me.

I see it all now. The whole ugly shape of it.

Brick didn't just betray the club. He betrayed me specifically.

Made me the sacrificial lamb. Sent me to prison to buy himself time. Then sold out to the Feds the moment I was locked up and couldn't question it.

And when I came home... he gave me my patch. Branded me. Made it permanent.

Not as a reward.

As a leash.

So when the time came—when he needed another scapegoat, another fall guy, another Kane to throw on the pyre—I'd already be tied down. Already branded. Already fuckin' owned.

Twenty-five thousand dollars.

Might as well be a million. Might as well be a bullet in the skull.

It's the same message either way: *Submit or die.*

The engine roars. Wind tears at my cut.

I think about Savannah. About her poem. Her certainty.

We'll build our kingdom from the ash and pain.

She's not backing down. Not letting the world dictate who she loves or where she belongs. She chose me. Keeps choosin' me. Every time I give her an out, she doubles down instead. Got my name inked on her skin. Swallowed my cock in front of forty-seven men. Let me fuck her rough, and leave marks, and call her mine while treating her like property.

And still she rides back to the silo. Still she writes me poems. Still she looks at me like I'm worth saving. If she's that sure—that committed—then what the fuck am I doing?

Running? Hiding? Waitin' for Brick to decide my fate?

No.

Fuck that.

Fuck Brick. Fuck the Feds. Fuck the whole rotted-out corpse of what the Badlands used to be.

Savannah's right. We carved this world from stone. Fire and blood. Condemned souls who refuse to stay down.

Let them come with their judgment and chains.

I'll burn it all before I let them take what's mine.

I'm done running from the hell I created.

Time to walk straight into it and make them remember who I am.

My name is Legion.

And I'm not rollin' over for anyone.

CHAPTER 7

LEGION

The eastern Montana badlands rise up around me like God's graveyard—ancient spires of eroded sandstone carved by wind and time into shapes that don't make sense. Red rock striations glow silver under the moon. Deep gullies cut between formations like open wounds in the earth's skin.

This land doesn't forgive.

Doesn't offer second chances or soft places to land.

It just is. Brutal, and honest, and unashamed of what it's become.

I get that. Understand it in my bones.

The bike eats up highway, then dirt road, then the unmarked two-track that leads to the compound. Dust plumes behind me in the headlight's wash. The air tastes like sage, and diesel, and something older—minerals, maybe. Stone ground down to powder over millennia.

Out here, you see what everything becomes eventually.

Dust, and silence, and wind that never stops.

The gate appears ahead, chain-link and razor wire catching moonlight. Two prospects lean against the guard shack, cigarettes glowing orange in the dark.

I slow. Stop.

Neither one meets my eyes.

Dusty shifts his weight. Crow stares at his boots like they're suddenly fascinating.

The gate opens. No words exchanged. No acknowledgment.

Just the mechanical grind of the motor pulling it aside.

I ride through.

Behind me, it closes with a metallic clang that sounds too much like a cell door.

How long?

The question sits in my chest like a stone.

How long has Brick been running this operation for the Feds?

Two years of nomads who aren't nomads. Two years of brothers voting on club business with federal prosecutors pulling their strings from the shadows.

Two years of lies, stacked on lies until the whole structure's rotten.

And how many men here hate it? How many are as pissed as I am about bein' used like pawns in somebody else's game?

I park the bike in its usual spot. Kill the engine.

The silence that follows feels heavy. Weighted with all the questions I can't ask and all the answers I already know.

However many men are angry, it's not enough.

Not enough to stand with me tomorrow when Brick calls church and demands his twenty-five-thousand-dollar blood price.

Not enough to vote against a president who's already proven he'll sell out anyone to protect his own skin.

Not enough to matter.

I pull off my helmet. Hang it on the handlebar.

The clubhouse squats ahead—cinderblock and corrugated steel, lights bleeding through dirty windows. Normally at this hour, there'd be noise. Music. Voices. The low rumble of brothers who can't sleep congregating in the bar to drink away whatever demons chase them.

Tonight—nothing.

Just the wind moving through the compound like a ghost looking for somewhere to haunt.

I push through the front door.

The bar's empty.

Completely empty.

No Diesel nursing a beer. No Chains sketching at a corner table. No prospects cleaning up or hanging around hoping to catch scraps of conversation that might teach them how to survive here.

Just empty tables. Stale air. The neon beer signs buzzing their lonely electric prayers into the dark.

In all my years at Badlands—prospect days, prison, coming home, getting patched—I've never seen this room empty.

Not once.

Paranoia crawls up my spine like something with too many legs.

Are they having a vote without me?

The thought hits sharp and cold. A secret church session where they decide my fate before I even walk through the door tomorrow.

I turn. Head back outside. Cross the compound toward the church building—the original structure, older than everything else here, where real club business gets handled.

The door's locked. No sound, no clues, just nothing.

I step back. Light a cigarette with hands that want to shake but won't let themselves.

Maybe everyone's asleep. Maybe it's late enough that even the insomniacs and addicts have given up and crawled into beds, or couches, or wherever the fuck they pass out.

Or maybe they're avoiding me.

Maybe I'm already dead, and they just haven't figured out how to tell me yet.

"Fuck it," I mutter to the empty compound.

I head for the bunkhouse. Climb the exterior stairs to the second floor. The hallway's dark except for one flickering overhead light that's been dying for six months. Nobody's fixed it. Nobody's going to.

Room 3. I open the door. Step inside. Close it behind me.

The space greets me the same way it always does—bare, and spartan, and deliberately free of anythin' that might make it feel like home.

Steel bed frame. Thin mattress. Gun rack bolted to the wall. Duffel bag in the corner containing everything I own that matters.

I strip off my cut. Hang it carefully on the hook by the door.

The brand underneath aches. Always aches now, even weeks after the infection. Scar tissue pulling wrong. Shape distorted where they cut away too much dead flesh trying to save my life.

I peel off my shirt. The B is barely recognizable. Just a mess of scars that burn when I move. Then the jeans. Kick them into the corner.

The shower's cramped, but it's better than nothin'. I turn the water on. Step under the spray before it's even warm. The cold water hits like a baptism.

I stand there. Let it pour over my head. Down my back. Washing away road dust, and Savannah's perfume, and the residue of every choice I've made that led me here.

If I could go back—

The thought rises unbidden.

If I could start over. Be fourteen again. Before Eleanor really got to me. Before she haunted my mind with truths and consequences. Before the club. Before I convinced myself that power and brotherhood were the only things worth having.

Would I do it different?

I press my forehead against the tile.

Yeah.

Yeah, I would.

I'd take Savannah's hand that first day in the silo and tell her the truth. That I already loved her. That I'd always love her. That whatever happened, she was the only good thing I'd ever touch.

I'd keep my distance from Badlands. From Brick's

offers, and Diesel's knowing looks, and the magnetic pull of belonging to something bigger than myself.

I'd work honest jobs. Save money. Buy that farmhouse she imagines when she's riding me slow and looking at me like I'm the answer to prayers she didn't know she was saying.

At the very least, I'd make myself something she could take home. A man who wouldn't embarrass her. I'd be the man she deserves, instead of the demon she settled for.

But I can't go back.

Can't undo the choices that carved me into this shape.

Can only stand here under cold water and wish I was someone else.

The water turns warm. Then hot. I scrub myself clean with bar soap that smells like nothing. Rinse. Turn off the spray and dry off with a towel that's rough from too many industrial washings. Then I pull on the only clean sweats I've got left—gray, worn soft, hanging low on my hips.

Back in the main room, I dig through my jeans pocket until I find the pack of cigarettes. Shake one loose. Light it up and lie down on the bed.

Then… I stare at the ceiling.

I smoke.

Ash into the empty beer can on the nightstand.

Try to sleep.

Can't.

Tomorrow changes everything.

One way or another, when dawn church convenes,

and Brick calls my name, and asks if I've got his money—

Which I don't, so…

So what. What's gonna happen tomorrow? I haven't really let myself think about it, but obviously, the fine is a way to get me to cave. To accept the rats and work for them. Spy, or whatever the fuck it is they're doing.

That's how fines work. You pay, one way or the other. If a brother owes a fine and misses his deadline, depending on the amount, he might get roughed up a bit or he might get put in the ground.

Twenty-five grand is an obscene amount of money to owe.

I roll over. Try to find a position that doesn't make the brand ache. My elbow hits something.

I freeze, my hand closing around something hard and lumpy beneath the pillow—something that definitely wasn't there the last time I was in this bed.

"What the fuck…" My voice comes out rough, edged with exhaustion and suspicion. It better not be a goddamn mouse that crawled under there to die, or I swear to Christ I'll burn this whole bed.

I sit up fully, joints protesting the movement, and reach back under the pillow with more purpose this time. My fingers find fabric and I pull it out into the dim light filtering through the blinds.

A drawstring sack. Canvas. Worn smooth at the edges like it's been used before, handled plenty. And heavy.

My pulse kicks up a notch as I work the drawstring loose with fingers that suddenly don't feel quite steady.

The mouth of the sack opens, and I tilt it toward the weak light coming from the security lights outside.

Stacks of twenties. Banded tight with those little paper wraps.

I dump the whole thing onto the mattress in front of me, watching the stacks tumble and scatter across the rumpled sheets. My hands move automatically, separating them, lining them up, fingers rifling through the edges to count. My brain's already doing the math before I'm halfway through.

Already know what the total's gonna be before I finish the last stack.

Twenty-five thousand dollars.

Exactly.

I count it again just to be sure. Separate the stacks. Hundreds mixed in with the twenties to make the math work.

$25,000.

My fine. My blood price. My Get-Out-of-Consequences-Free card.

There's a note in the bottom of the sack.

I unfold it.

Typed. Block letters. Nothing handwritten. Nothing that could be traced back to whoever put this here.

Three words:

GOT YOU TOMORROW.

I stare at it.

Read it again.

Got you tomorrow.

Could mean: I've got your back. I'm covering you. You're safe because someone paid your debt.

Could mean: I've got you trapped. You owe me now. This isn't freedom—it's a different kind of leash.

Could mean: I've got plans for you. This money buys your life, but it also buys your loyalty. And you'll pay it back in ways you won't see coming until it's too late.

Could mean: I've got faith in you. Fight tomorrow. Survive tomorrow. This is just the first move in a longer game.

Could mean: I've got nothing to lose. If you go down, I go down. So here's a lifeline. Use it or don't— but know that someone's willing to burn their own resources to keep you breathing.

I turn the note over.

Nothing on the back.

No signature. No clue.

Just those three words that could be salvation or damnation depending on who left them.

Diesel?

He said he had my back. But twenty-five grand is serious money. More than most brothers keep liquid. More than you hand over without expecting something in return.

Savannah?

She's got access to that kind of cash. But she doesn't know about the fine. I didn't tell her. Didn't want to drag her into club business.

Brick?

Fuck, what if this is a test? What if he wants to see if I'll take the money or refuse it on principle? What if paying the fine with mystery cash just digs me deeper into whatever hole he's already planning?

Someone else entirely?

A brother I don't know as well. Someone who sees the same rot I see and wants an ally when the reckoning comes.

Or a Fed wearing a cut, buying my cooperation with cash that disappeared from an evidence locker without anyone noticing.

I pick up one of the stacks. Flip through the bills.

All real. All used enough to have been in circulation. Nothing sequential. Nothing that screams trap.

Just money.

Twenty-five thousand reasons to shut up, and show up tomorrow, and hand Brick exactly what he asked for.

I set it down. Light another cigarette.

The note stares at me from the mattress.

Got you tomorrow.

Promise or threat.

Salvation or sentence.

I won't know until tomorrow which one it is.

I lie back down. Money scattered around me like some fucked-up parody of wealth.

Smoke rises toward the ceiling. It curls in the air currents, a draft from the broken window I never fixed.

Outside, the compound's still silent.

No brothers drinking. No music. No voices raised in argument or laughter.

Just wind. Just distance. Just the space between breaths where everything waits.

I don't sleep.

Can't sleep.

Just lie there watching the ceiling while the hours drain away.

Thinking about Savannah's poem. About her certainty. About the way she looked at me in the silo like I was still worth saving despite all the evidence to the contrary.

Thinking about Mercy at Rimrock. Safe. Happy. Finally getting the childhood she deserves.

Thinking about Diesel's warning. About Brick's betrayal. About forty-seven men who sold their souls in different increments to different devils.

Thinking about the money scattered on my bed and the note that won't tell me who to trust.

The only thing I know is that when the sun clears the horizon, I'll walk into church with twenty-five thousand dollars I didn't earn.

And then... I'll find out exactly what it costs me.

CHAPTER 8
SAVANNAH

I ride home slow.

Cassia knows something's wrong. She keeps turning her head like she's checking on me, ears flicking backward to catch my mood.

I'm not crying.

Should be, maybe. But I'm too busy replaying every second of what just happened at the silo.

The way Legion touched me. Rough, yes. Desperate, absolutely.

But underneath all of it—underneath the commands and the dirty talk and the way he used my body like he was trying to prove something—there was goodbye threaded through every thrust.

I liked it.

That's not the problem.

I liked how rough he was. Liked being degraded, and claimed, and fucked like I was the only thing keeping him tethered to earth.

The problem is I don't know why.

Why tonight felt different.

Why he needed me that way right now.

Why he apologized after—called himself filthy and me clean when we both know better.

Something happened.

Something he decided not to tell me about.

And I let him fuck me instead of demanding answers.

Cassia's hooves hit the dirt in steady rhythm. Four-beat walk. Slow and unhurried because I'm in no rush to get back.

I lean forward slightly, stroking her neck.

"I'm a coward," I tell her.

She snorts. Doesn't disagree.

Because I am.

Legion was spiraling right in front of me and I chose to let him deflect with nostalgia and sex instead of pushing him to tell me the truth.

Why should he tell me anything?

What have I actually done to earn that kind of trust?

The thought settles heavy in my chest. Makes it hard to breathe.

I saved his life—but that was selfish. Pure fucking selfishness.

He was dying and I threw money at doctors because I couldn't bear to lose him. Couldn't imagine waking up in a world where Legion Kane wasn't breathing.

That wasn't generosity.

That was survival instinct.

I needed him alive the same way I need air.

And Mercy…

God, I can't even take credit there.

Cash did everything.

Cash got her away from the clubhouse when social services came knocking.

Cash brought her to the ranch and gave her a bedroom bigger than the entire trailer she grew up in.

Cash bought her the puppy.

Cash paid for the new clothes, the riding lessons with Madeline, the private tutors to catch her up before school started.

It was Cash's idea to enroll her at Rimrock.

Not mine.

I just... went along with it. Smiled and played nice aunt while my brother actually changed that little girl's entire life.

Mercy's thriving because of him.

Not me.

So what have I actually done?

What have I given Legion besides my body and my certainty that I want him?

Cassia's ears flick back again.

I straighten in the saddle, loosening my grip on the reins.

"Sorry, girl."

She huffs. Keeps walking.

The night air smells like sage and dust. Storm's still building somewhere to the east but it hasn't reached us yet.

I think about Eleanor.

Can't help it.

Think about the safe room deep underground. The old bank vault surrounded by cinderblocks. The red leather album inside.

The Book of Legion.

I should tell him it exists. Not ask about it. Not demand explanations or confessions. Just... let him know.

Hey, by the way, my dead mother kept a private archive of thousands of photographs she took of you from the time you were a toddler until six months before she died. Some of them are you as a child. Some are you and me as teenagers kissing. And some are professional studio portraits of you half-naked looking sad, and beautiful, and broken.

Also there's a selfie of the two of you together looking comfortable and happy, dated six months before her death, when you were twenty-four and I was at college and you definitely never mentioned knowing her that well.

Just thought you should know.

My stomach twists.

Finding that book destroyed something in me.

I remember standing in the safe room with the album open in my hands, flipping through page after page of Legion's face.

My heart hurt.

Physically hurt.

Like someone reached into my chest and squeezed until I couldn't breathe.

Because I knew what it meant.

Eleanor was obsessed with him.

The same way she was obsessed with creating the perfect Savannah Ashby brand. The same way she controlled every aspect of my childhood and turned me into content.

She did something to Legion too.

I don't know what. Don't know if I want to know.

But whatever happened between them—

God, maybe that's why I never fully committed to the idea of us.

Maybe some part of me felt like I could never measure up to her.

Eleanor with her talent, and vision, and terrifying certainty about everything she touched.

How could I compete with that?

How could I be enough for Legion when my own mother saw something in him worth documenting obsessively for twenty-five years?

Cassia stumbles slightly on loose rock.

I automatically adjust my seat, keeping her balanced.

"Easy, girl." She recovers. Keeps walking.

The stables come into view ahead. Dark shapes against darker landscape.

I take a breath. Let it out slow.

Whatever happened between Eleanor and Legion— it's none of my business. I've come to terms with that now.

Or I'm trying to.

Because the truth is… Legion Kane is the only man I want. Not Marcus with his political ambitions and cold calculation. Not some fantasy of who Legion could be if he wasn't who he is.

Just him.

The real him.

Rough, and damaged, and dangerous, and mine.

But he's not going to trust me with his secrets if I keep taking without giving.

If I keep letting him deflect and dodge and carry

everything alone.

I need to change.

Need to be more present in his life.

Need to show him I'm with him—not because he's my rebellion, or my project, or my way of escaping the Ashby cage.

But because I choose him. Every day. Even when it's hard.

Especially, when it's hard.

Cassia and I reach the stable yard. I slide off her back, my legs shaky from the ride and everything else, then lead her inside. The barn smells like hay, and leather, and horse. It's familiar and grounding.

I unsaddle her, brush her down, check her hooves. She leans into the grooming, content.

"You're a good girl," I murmur. Better than me, probably.

When she's settled in her stall with fresh water and hay, I close the door and head toward the house. The mansion looms ahead. Every window dark except the kitchen where we leave a light on all night.

I slip inside and walk barefoot through halls I've known my entire life. Up the back staircase to the second floor, down the hallway to my room.

Inside, I close the door and lean against it.

What can I change right now?

What can I do tonight to show Legion I'm serious?

That I'm here. That I'm not going anywhere. That he can trust me with whatever's breaking him apart.

I cross to the bathroom. Strip out of the white dress that still smells like him—smoke, and leather, and sex—

and then pull on a pair of sleep shorts and an old t-shirt. I wash my face and brush my teeth.

Then… I stare at myself in the mirror.

I look like exactly what I am.

A woman who got thoroughly fucked outside an abandoned grain silo by a man she'd burn the world for.

I turn away from my reflection, walk back into the bedroom, grab my phone from the nightstand, and open Instagram without letting myself think about it too much.

My account stares back at me. Four point two million followers. Hundreds of unread messages. Thousands of comments I haven't looked at in weeks.

I haven't posted since I was kidnapped by my fiancée and everything I thought I knew about this world turned out to be a lie.

I create a post. Don't bother adding a photo, it's not that kind of post. And then… I start typing.

I know there are rumors. So let's address them.

Delete that. Too defensive.

Some of you have questions about my engagement.

Delete. Too vague.

I close my eyes.

Think about Legion in the silo. The way he held me after. The way he thanked me for things I didn't deserve credit for.

The way he looked at me like I was something precious, even while calling himself filthy.

Open my eyes.

Type.

I know there are questions. Rumors. Speculation about

what those videos mean, and who I am, and what happens next.

So let me try to answer them—not because I owe explanations, but because for once in my life, I want to tell the truth without a filter between my heart and my words.

Marcus and I are no longer together. He ended our engagement after those videos surfaced, and I don't blame him. Not even a little.

It's a lie, but it needs to be this way.

He deserves someone who can love him wholly, completely, without reservation. And I can't. Because my heart has belonged to someone else since I was twelve years old, since before I understood what it meant to give your heart away and never ask for it back.

I pause.

Stare at the words.

Legion would hate being named. Hate being dragged into my Instagram drama.

But I need to explain thoroughly, so there is no misunderstanding. So I keep typing.

I've been in love with the same man for eighteen years. Through day school, boarding school, college. All of it. Through the death of my mother and all the many, many years we spent apart.

There is no time, no distance, no consequence that could make me stop loving him.

It was him I was thinking about during every carefully staged photo and through a staged engagement that looked perfect on camera but felt like death waiting to happen.

I've loved this man in secret, in silence, in the spaces between the life I was performing and the life I was actually living.

Another pause.

This feels right.

Feels honest in a way nothing else I've posted has been in years.

If you've been here a while, you know my mother built something extraordinary. A brand. An empire. A vision of ranch life that was equal parts authentic and aspirational—heritage, and beauty, and the mythology of the American West wrapped in golden hour light and perfect composition. And when she died, I inherited all of it. The land, the legacy, the responsibility of maintaining the image she spent decades building.

I learned to perform it well. Maybe too well. Turned my whole life into content, into aesthetic, into something pretty enough to sell. Ranch princess living. Heritage homesteading. The girl in the white dress on horseback with wildflowers in her hair.

But here's the truth I should have said years ago: you don't need me to live the life you want.

The ranch aesthetic, the homesteading movement, the whole #WildRanchLife community—you've taken it so much further than I ever could. You're out there actually living it. Raising your chickens, and baking your bread, and learning to ride, and building something real with your hands, and your hearts, and your stubborn, beautiful determination.

I was just showing you a prettier, more polished version of what you're already doing.

And I think... I think maybe it's time I stopped performing and started living too.

The man I love doesn't fit the narrative people expected for my life. He's rough where I'm polished. He's complicated, and messy, and nothing like the safe, respectable choice.

But he's mine.

He's been mine since we were teenagers hiding in an old abandoned grain silo, talking until sunrise about dreams we didn't have words for yet. And I'm choosing him. I'm choosing us. I'm choosing the kind of love that doesn't need to be staged, or curated, or filtered through a lens.

The kind that just… is.

So this account is going quiet for now. Not gone—I'm not disappearing. But I'm not performing anymore either. If something happens worth sharing, something real, and joyful, and true, I'll let you know.

But I'm done turning my life into content. Done editing my feelings into captions. Done being Savannah Ashby, the brand.

I just want to be Savannah. The girl who fell in love at twelve years old and never quite fell back out.

Thank you for being part of this journey. For letting me into your homes and hearts. For building something so much more beautiful and authentic than anything I showed you.

Keep going. Keep building. Keep living.

You're already doing everything right.

With all my love,

Savannah

I hit post before I can second-guess it. Then I wait, watching it go live.

The engagement starts immediately. Likes flooding in. Comments loading.

I don't read them.

Just set the phone face-down on the nightstand, turn off the light, snuggle into my bed, pull the covers up, and stare at the ceiling.

My heart's pounding like I just did something terrifying.

Maybe I did.

Just blew up my entire carefully curated image.

Confirmed the worst rumors.

Admitted to being in love with someone who isn't my politically connected ex-fiancé.

Told four million strangers I'm choosing messy over perfect.

Real over pretty.

Legion over everything.

The room's quiet except for the ceiling fan and my breathing.

Tomorrow, Cash will probably have opinions.

Wyatt will make drunk comments.

Marcus will rage, and stomp his feet, and make threats.

My followers will either support me or unfollow in droves.

Tomorrow, there will be consequences.

But tonight—

Tonight I chose something for myself.

Chose to be honest about wanting Legion even if it costs me everything else.

That's a start. Not trust earned, maybe. But a step toward earning it. Toward being someone he can actually lean on instead of someone he has to protect from the truth.

I close my eyes and let exhaustion pull me under.

Sleep finds me thinking about Legion's hands on my body.

About the way he said he loved me.

About tomorrow, and the next day, and all the days after that.

About becoming someone who deserves the words he won't say out loud but shows me every time he touches me like I'm the only real thing in his world.

About being present.

Being there.

Being enough.

It's... enough.

CHAPTER 9
LEGION

I wake to the sound of nothing.

No boots on the stairs. No voices through the walls. No engine rumble from the lot. Just silence—heavy and wrong, like the compound's holding its breath.

Gray light bleeds through dirty blinds, cutting stripes across the concrete floor. The steel bed frame creaks when I shift, the metal protesting under my weight.

The canvas bag sits on the floor beside my duffel. Twenty-five thousand dollars. I stare at it from the bed, one arm behind my head, breathing shallow in the quiet.

Got you tomorrow.

I sit up slow, my feet hittin' the cold floor. The shock of it travels up through my bones, waking me fully. I dress in jeans and a t-shirt. Then I pull the Glock 19 from under my pillow. The grip fits my palm like it was molded there. I check the magazine—fifteen rounds staring back at me, then chamber a round with a metallic click that echoes in the small room.

The sound is honest.

I tuck the gun in my waistband at the small of my back, under where my cut will hang so it won't print. Hidden but accessible. I've carried it this way a thousand times, but today feels like all of those moments collapsed into one.

I shoulder into my cut. Enjoying the way the leather settles across my shoulders, weight distributed the way it's supposed to be. The Badlands patch is visible in the mirror beside my bed—skull wrapped in barbed wire, rising from cracked earth. My demon name stitched below it in white thread.

I sigh, then look away from my reflection. Don't need to see what I already know.

Then I pick up the money bag. Loop the drawstring around my wrist. It's a prop. Theatre. Something to carry so my hands look occupied, so they think I'm playing along.

I'm not paying the fine.

I leave my room.

The door closes behind me with a soft click. I walk down the hallway, then the stairs, then outside. The compound spreads out before me, the morning sun already hot. With every step, the dust rises, coating my boots in fine powder as I take in the nomad bikes all lined up in formation near the church entrance.

Brandy follows me out, plants herself on the porch, and leans against a railing with a phone against her ear. Spyin' on me, I guess. Not even tryin' to hide it.

I don't acknowledge her. Don't even let my eyes

linger. She's a Fed, or she's handling Brick, or she's both, and none of it matters because in ten minutes she'll be irrelevant.

I notice other details as I walk.

No prospects. No hangarounds. The usual morning traffic of women, and workers, and members grabbing breakfast—nothin'. The compound feels emptied out in a deliberate way.

I reach the heavy steel church door, pausing at the threshold.

I take one breath. Hold it. Let it out slow.

This is instinct now. No plan. No speech rehearsed. Just action. Pure and simple.

The way it's always been with me.

I step inside.

The room comes into focus in one sweep.

Brick at the head table, center position. Gray beard. Cold eyes downcast, looking at the papers spread in front of him like he's conducting legitimate business. Roach to his left—twitchy hands already drumming on the table. Ledger to his right, glasses reflecting fluorescent light, calculator face giving nothing away.

Officers flanking. Patched members in their seats arranged in rows. Everybody's early, it seems.

Weird.

But I'm beyond carin'.

The nomads are grouped at the back. Standing. Hands in their pocket's or crossed in front of their chests, like they belong here.

Like they own the place. Because they do. Have for two years now, according to Diesel.

Brick looks up from his papers. Eyes lock on mine.

Expression unreadable—not surprised, not angry, not pleased. Just waiting. Calculating.

"Right on time," he says. Voice casual but eyes sharp. "Got something for me, Demon?"

I walk forward. Slow. Deliberate. The money bag swings slightly in my left hand with each step.

Men turn to watch me pass. I notice positions without looking directly at anyone.

Diesel sittin' next to Ledger at the front. Havoc in the middle of all the other patched members. His eyes track me, but his face is blank. Chains and Ratchet are together on the left.

I reach the table, five feet from Brick. Close enough to see the gray threadin' through his beard and the calculation in his eyes. His fingers rest flat on the papers, all casual and controlled like this isn't a fuckin' set up to ruin my life.

I set the bag down on the scarred wood. Don't let go of it yet, just let it rest there between us.

Brick reaches for it.

My right hand moves to my back. Smooth. Practiced. No hesitation. No thought between intention and action. I find the grip, my fingers closin' around it, and I pull the gun out in one fluid motion.

I draw, raise, extend, sight, breathe.

Then I shoot Brick between the eyes. Point-blank range. Maybe four feet. Can't miss at this distance even if I wanted to.

The sound is massive in the enclosed space. A deafening crack that punches through my eardrums and keeps echoing, bouncing off the cinderblock walls.

Brick's body snaps backward. His head whipping

back so hard, I hear vertebrae crack. There's a small entry wound—just a dark hole punched through his forehead, almost neat. The back is another matter altogether. Skull fragments. Brain bits. Blood spray painting the memorial photos on the wall behind him.

Then he drops. Just collapses like someone cut his strings. His chair goes over backward, his body hits the concrete, and… that's it.

Over.

The room *freezes*.

Total silence except for my ears ringing. Half a second that stretches into eternity. Every man stunned into stillness, their hands frozen mid-gesture, their mouths open and eyes wide. Cigarettes burn between fingers, forgotten.

Nobody breathes.

I pivot. Gun already tracking. My body moving on autopilot. I find the nearest nomad. The one with the shaved head and tribal tattoos snaking up his neck. He's reaching for his weapon. Too slow. Way too slow.

I fire. Center mass. Double tap. Two rounds punched through his white T-shirt before he clears leather. Red blooms across the cotton like flowers opening. He staggers backward, his mouth workin' like a fish as he tries to breathe through punctured lungs. Then he goes down with a crash.

Chaos erupts. Everyone moves at once. Chairs scrape against the floor, shouts are overlapping— warnings, curses, names being screamed. The unmistakable sound of weapons being drawn from leather, slides racking, safeties clicking off.

Men look around wildly.

Guns out but nobody knows who to aim at. We're all wearing the same patch. Same cuts. Same colors. Same fucking brotherhood that Brick sold to the Feds two years ago.

Confusion in every face.

Which is exactly what I need.

I find the second nomad—the one with the goatee and the custom leather gloves. He's faster than the first. Gun already out. Raising it. Finger on the trigger.

I shoot him in the head. Clean shot. Top of the skull. He drops before his gun finishes its arc upward. His body crumples as skull fragments scatter across concrete like shrapnel.

A gunshot explodes up front.

I turn. Diesel.

He's standing, gun drawn, face set in that expression I've seen before—the one that says he made his choice before walking in this room. Takes down the third nomad before anyone processes what's happening. Chest shot. Dead center. The nomad spins from the impact. Falls across a chair. Doesn't get back up.

Another shot—Havoc.

Standing now. Braced against his chair. Fourth nomad drops. Throat shot. Blood sprays in an arterial arc across two rows of seats. Choking sounds. Hands clawing at his neck as he goes down, trying to hold his life inside and failing.

Chains and Ratchet open up simultaneously.

Synchronized like they planned it. Like they talked about this. Like they knew.

Someone tries to run for the exit. Big mistake. It's a

younger guy, younger than me, who doesn't live here. Only came in for the vote.

Probably another fuckin' Fed. He makes it three steps before taking a bullet in the shoulder from Chains. It spins him around, then he takes another from Ratchet, it spins him back.

Time is movin' in fragments now.

Diesel shooting. Havoc shooting. Chains and Ratchet. Nobody hesitating. My people knew. They were ready. They made this choice before the door even opened.

All the rats drop in seconds.

The room goes quiet again. Just for a heartbeat. Just long enough for everyone to realize what just happened. Heavy breathing. Gunsmoke hanging thick in fluorescent light. The chemical taste of burnt powder coating my tongue.

Then Ledger moves.

His chair crashes backward and then he's on his feet, aimin' at me. His finger's on the trigger and his face is twistin' with rage, or fear, or calculation—can't tell which.

Diesel shoots him before he can fire.

Ledger's shoulder explodes. Red mist. Bone fragments. He spins from the impact, gun dropping from nerveless fingers. Goes to his knees. Mouth open. Eyes wide and shocked like he can't believe his own brother just shot him.

"Diesel—" he starts.

Nobody lets him finish.

Roach lunges for cover behind the overturned table.

Scrambling. Desperate. He reaches for a gun on the

floor—Brick's gun, dropped when he fell. His fingers are stretching for it when Chains shoots him from the side.

Back of the head. Clean shot. No drama. Roach goes limp mid-reach. Body settling against the table leg like he's just resting. Blood pools under his cheek.

Club members start choosin' sides in real time.

Some dive behind overturned chairs. Some freeze completely, caught between loyalty and survival. Some raise weapons and fire. The room divides along invisible lines everyone suddenly understands—Brick's people versus Legion's people. Traitors versus loyal. Feds versus Badlands.

The real Badlands.

Bullets fly in every direction.

Muzzle flashes lighting up the dim room like strobe lights. Brass casings hitting concrete with metallic pings, rolling, scattering. Men screamin'—warnings, curses, names. "Get down!" "Behind you!" "Fuck—"

The sound is overwhelmin'.

A member on Brick's side—I recognize him, rode with him, don't remember his name—shoots at Diesel from behind a chair. Misses. Round punches through the cinderblock wall behind him, showering dust.

Diesel doesn't flinch. Returns fire without hesitation. Two shots. Both hit. The member drops, slides down the wall leaving a red smear.

Another traitor tries to run for the door.

Ratchet cuts him down before he's halfway across the room. Three rounds in the back. Tight grouping. The man's momentum carries him forward even as his legs give out. He slides down the door, leaving a red smear on the steel.

Havoc provides cover fire from behind the overturned church table. Kneeling. Braced. Methodical shots. Taking his time. Picking targets. Breathing between rounds like he's at the range teaching prospects. Like this is just another drill.

A bullet catches him in the chest. Right side. I see it hit, watching as his body rocks backward, his face twistin'.

But he keeps shooting. Doesn't go down. Just adjusts his position. Shifts weight. Keeps firing like the bullet was an inconvenience, not a wound.

Another round hits his shoulder. Left side this time. His gun wavers, but doesn't drop. Blood soaking his cut, spreading dark across the leather. Face going pale, but jaw set. Still shooting.

A third bullet strikes him in the neck. It's over. Blood sprays across the table he's using for cover. Across his hands. Across the floor. His gun falls. He goes down hard, his body hitting the floor with a sound I'll hear forever.

The fighting intensifies after Havoc falls. There's no reason to be measured or cautious. This is a hunt, and we're pickin' off traitors one by one. Bodies dropping every few seconds, blood pooling and spreading as the floor becomes slick with it. Shell casing's are everywhere.

I empty my gun into a traitor trying to flank until the magazine locks back empty—the slide frozen. Another mag slips in on instinct.

A traitor rushes me while I'm reloading. Close

quarters. Desperate. No gun. Just hands reaching for my throat. Eyes wild. Mouth open in a scream I can't hear over the ringing in my ears.

I finish the reload. Bring the gun up. Shoot him in the face. Point-blank. The body drops at my feet. Blood and bone fragments spray across my jeans.

The last traitor standing drops his weapon.

Hands up. Shaking. Mouth open. Eyes wide. About to beg, or bargain, or offer something.

Diesel shoots him anyway.

No hesitation. No mercy. No prisoners.

The gunfire stops abruptly.

Like someone shut off a switch. Like the world ran out of bullets and violence all at once.

Ringing silence. Everyone's ears are screamin'. The gunsmoke's thick enough to taste.

Someone pounds on the door from outside.

Fists hammering as muffled voices carry through the steel. The prospects, or the women, demandin' to know what happened.

The door is barred from the inside. They don't have a chance in hell of gettin' in.

I count the standing men.

Diesel—cut soaked with someone else's blood, breathing hard. Face spattered with red. Gun still in hand.

Chains—smoking gun still raised. Glass eye reflecting fluorescent light. Real eye tracking the bodies.

Ratchet—reloading methodically. Checking his magazine. Counting rounds like this is just another day.

Four, five, six… twenty-two patched members still breathing, including me.

The body count, on the other hand, is a shit-show of a number. The church looks like a slaughterhouse.

Diesel steps forward into the center of the room, then points at the survivors. "You stand for Badlands or you die with them," he says. "Right fucking now. Not to Legion. Not to me. To *Badlands*. The real Badlands. Not Brick's Fed operation. Not some rat deal. The patch. The brotherhood. The life."

He's not asking permission or takin' a fuckin' vote.

He wants a pledge and he wants it now. Normally, I'd say this was not a great way to total up your loyal members. With bodies and blood pooling in the room, still wet.

But they're alive for a reason and all of them are holding weapons.

They don't hesitate. They declare one by one.

"Badlands."

"Badlands."

"Badlands."

Down the line until everyone's spoken except me.

I don't need to say it. They already know. But I do anyway. "It's only ever been Badlands."

Diesel nods. "Welp," he starts. Like this is just another day in the life. "You're in charge now, Legion." He looks at the rest of us. "Anyone got a problem with that?"

They shake their heads.

"Good," Diesel says. Then he pushes his bloody knuckles at me. "All hail, President Demon."

I blow out a breath, dap him, then stand there like an idiot as all the other guys follow his lead.

When that's over, I look at Chains, who is kneeling

beside Havoc's body. He's careful and respectful as he presses two fingers to his neck. Checking for a pulse even though it's obvious. He waits. Finds nothing. Then looks up and meets my eyes. "Gone."

I think about June. Their farmhouse. Their dinner table. Their six kids. The way she looked at Havoc like he was her whole world.

Time for that sorrow later.

Right now, we're still in the middle of winning.

"OK," I say, pointing at the door. Outside, people are still bangin'. "We got things to take care of out there too."

Diesel nods to me.

I nod back.

Then I turn to Ratchet. "Open it."

Ratchet pulls the steel crossbeam. He yanks it free with both hands and lets it clang to the floor. The sound echoes as he pulls the door open. The hinges protest with a long shriek as sunlight floods in.

I step out first. Smoke billowing out behind me like I'm walking through fog. Gun still in hand, eyes adjusting to brightness. The compound spreads before me—bikes, buildings, dust, sky.

Brandy starts toward me, twenty feet away. Moving fast. Mouth opening. About to speak. Phone still clutched in her hand. Eyes wide—fear, or surprise, or calculation.

I raise my gun without breaking stride. Her death comes smooth. One shot, right between her eyes. She drops mid-step, slumping to the dirt. Her phone clatters as blood starts pooling under her blonde hair.

Silence.

I scan the immediate area. Five women outside in various positions. One near the garage—younger, probably early twenties. Two by the main clubhouse—hangarounds I recognize but don't know their names. One near the bikes—older, maybe thirties. One trying to back away—moving slow, hands up.

I look at Diesel without speaking, not asking.

And no one hesitates.

We all raise our weapons as one.

They're runnin' now. But it only takes five seconds to make the world go still again.

Six bodies, including Brandy. Which isn't really important. It's the people who aren't here, that matter.

They were told to stay away.

None of this was about me, or my fine. It wasn't even about Brick.

It was about loyalty. Principle.

It was a trap.

Silence settles over the compound.

Just wind. Dust devils spinning in the parking lot.

I spend the rest of the day feelin' nothin'. Hollow, where emotions should be. Because there's work to do. Bodies to bury, blood to mop up, things to work out. Practical matters that add up to survival logistics.

And the whole time I feel it.

Something has changed.

Everything has changed.

Because nothin' says you're all in like a massacre.

CHAPTER 10
LEGION

The golden hour washes over me as I ride. The wind is blowin' my hair, the sky all the colors of hell. Gorgeous bands of reds and purples softened up by deep peach and dark teal. A nightmare conjured up from the vacant mind of an insane artist.

Absolutely stunnin'. Unbelievably real. Indisputably foreboding.

There's no other way to interpret this sky.

Not after what happened this morning.

The body count felt like infinity, which was fitting. Because it seemed to take an eternity to bury them all. Even with the excavator, it was a chore.

The entire day felt like the definition of futility.

There's no fuckin' way we're gettin' away with this.

There's no fuckin' way this doesn't end in some televised shoot-out. The United States government vs. Badlands MC.

We're dead. We're all dead.

And I'm the one to blame for it.

Savannah is the only thing I care about right now. Who knows how long I have. Forty-eight hours? Seventy-two, if I'm lucky.

I've got things to say to that woman. Things that can't wait because this is it. The war is over. I've finally chosen my side. The archangel on my chest never had a chance. It's the screamin' demons that always had the upper hand. They always knew what truly lived inside me.

The Ashby Ranch rises up over the ridge like it always does. Perfect. Untouchable. Green grass that shouldn't exist in September, black fences that only people with money can really appreciate.

I slow the bike as I approach the gate. It's open.

Not quite dark yet, but almost. That in-between time when the world holds its breath.

She must hear me comin' because she's already on the porch when I round the last curve. Smilin'. White dress flowin' around her legs. Hair loose. Like a world that includes Demon Kane still exists.

Like I didn't just bury thirty-six bodies, includin' Havoc. Twenty-five traitors. Five Feds, includin' Brandy. And five women that were probably also Feds, but there was no way to sort that out, so... yeah. It is what it is.

I park the bike, kill the engine, and let the silence crash down. My leg comes over the bike slow, every muscle in my body screamin' from diggin' and draggin' corpses.

Savannah's smile drops the second she really sees me.

I know what she's lookin' at. The dirt caked into

every crease of my jeans—dark red Montana clay that looks too much like dried blood even though it's not. There's dust in my hair, on my face, streaking across my cut. My boots are covered in it. My fingernails black crescents.

She doesn't move toward me, just stands there, fifteen feet between us, her hand on the railing. "Legion." Her voice cracks. "What's wrong?"

I open my mouth. Close it. Blow out a breath and try again. But the words won't come out. How the fuck do I explain this? The death, the blood, the end.

Because that's what this is. The fuckin' end. Of everything. Me, me and her, the club, everyone still alive in the club. Families ruined today. June's a widow. Orphans, and women, and the whole fuckin' future of everyghing went up in ashes this morning.

No. Angels and ashes don't belong together. So I say, "There's this book. It's… red, I think." Like the blood all over the floor this morning. "Leather. I don't remember much about what it looked like, just… there's a *book*, Savannah. Your mama. She…"

I inhale. Exhale.

I have no idea how to explain this.

"Pictures," I finally manage. "Of me. Do you know what I'm talkin' about? Do you know where it is?"

I don't even know how to describe the look on Savannah's face. It's intense concentration wrapped around somethin' else—disbelief maybe, or acceptance, or both things wound together so tight you can't tell where one ends and the other begins. Her mouth opens slightly like she's gonna say somethin', then it closes. Her eyes search mine with this desperate, hungry need to understand what I'm askin' and why I'm askin' it now, covered in grave dirt and the residue of violence I can't wash off no matter how hard I scrub.

She knew.

She knows about this book. Has looked at it. Studied it probably. I can see the questions all over her face—questions about what Eleanor did, questions about what I let her do, questions about why I never mentioned it, why I never explained, why I kept silent about one more goddamn thing in a life already buried under secrets.

And she never once asked me about it.

Never brought it up. Never demanded answers. Never used it as a weapon the way she could've—the way anyone else would've.

That realization hits me harder than Brick's bullet would've if I'd been slower this mornin'. Harder than the knowledge that I just murdered the club president in cold blood and buried him in Montana clay that'll hold his bones forever.

She doesn't say nothin'. Just... extends her hand. Small. Delicate. Palm up. Offerin' herself as a guide through whatever fresh hell this day is about to become.

I walk forward and take it, and she leads me inside the mansion I lived in for weeks without ever really seein' it—without ever really believin' I belonged in a place this clean, this expensive, this far removed from the world I was born into.

We go up the stairs, her bare feet silent on the hardwood, my boots leaving evidence of evil with every step.

I follow her into her bedroom and for one horrible moment, I wonder if the book has been on some shelf in this room the whole time. Wonder if I walked past it dozens of times when I was livin' here, recoverin' from the infection that nearly killed me, driftin' through this house like a ghost who couldn't quite figure out how to haunt properly. Wonder if she kept it out in the open, displayed like a trophy, or a warning, or a confession she wanted me to find, but couldn't bring herself to speak aloud.

But it's not.

She takes me into her closet—this massive walk-in space bigger than Mercy's entire bedroom at the trailer —and in the back, behind rows and rows of prairie dresses in soft colors that make her look like some kind of virgin sacrifice, even though we both know better, there's a panel.

It slides open on her command, revealin' an elevator.

An elevator. In a closet. In a bedroom.

Of course there's a fuckin' elevator. Of course the Ashbys have secret passages, and hidden rooms, and layers upon layers of privacy built into their fortress. Of course Savannah grew up in a house where you could disappear into the walls, where you could hide from cameras, and expectations, and your own mother's obsessive need to document every breath you took.

Of course there is.

The elevator requires a key in the form of a code— numbers Savannah punches in without hesitation. We get in. The doors close. We descend.

The ride down feels longer than it probably is, and

I'm acutely aware of how small this space is. How Savannah's pressed against my side even though there's room to stand apart. How she's still holdin' my hand like she's afraid if she lets go, I'll disappear into the same abyss that swallowed Brick, and Roach, and Ledger, and all the others who thought they could survive by choosin' the wrong side today.

We exit.

And I step out into a shrine of photographs.

All of it, Eleanor's work. Everywhere. Floor to ceiling. Wall to wall. Thousands upon thousands of images preserved in climate-controlled perfection—negatives in archival sleeves, prints in acid-free boxes, contact sheets organized by date, and subject, and whatever system made sense inside Eleanor Ashby's brilliant, broken mind.

This is where she kept her real legacy. Not the Instagram empire. Not the coffee table books, or the magazine spreads, or the perfectly staged moments she sold to millions of followers who thought they were seein' authenticity.

This is where I end this day. I almost laugh. It's almost funny.

But none of this is funny.

None of this has ever been funny.

Back in time, I'm twenty-five years old and ridin' my bike into Glendive, Montana on a Thursday afternoon in September.

Eleanor's studio is in the quaint downtown. Sandwiched between the Yellowstone River and the train tracks. The buildin' is old, nondescript brick.

Single steel door. Number painted in faded white. I've been here before, obviously. Been coming to this place for seven years by the time this day comes around.

But it's different now. There's no sign anymore. Nothin' that says she's in there.

I kill the engine and sit there for a minute, smokin', wonderin' what the fuck I'm doin' here. Wonderin' why I keep comin' back every time she calls, every time she leaves a note on my bike, every time she drops another breadcrumb about my father. A man I never knew. A man I never wanted to know.

But I know why.

Because Eleanor's the only person who ever looked at me like I mattered. Like I'm somethin' worth preserving. Like my existence is evidence of beauty instead of evidence of sin.

I flick the cigarette into the street and walk inside.

The space opens up into somethin' that doesn't match the exterior at all. Professional photography studio. Lights on tall stands with umbrellas and softboxes, pristine white backdrops suspended from ceiling-mounted rails, camera equipment organized on rolling carts—everything precise, and deliberate, and expensive. The kind of setup photographers dream about.

And there's Eleanor.

She's thinner than she was last month. The change isn't dramatic. Yet. But it will be soon. Her face has this gaunt quality that wasn't there before, like somethin's consuming her from the inside out.

But she's smilin'.

Actually happy. Not the practiced Instagram smile

she wears for cameras, or the polite social mask she shows donors and politicians. Real happiness. The kind that lights a person up from within, the kind that makes her look younger despite everything that's tryin' to eat her alive.

And I realize—standin' there in my jeans and leather jacket, smellin' like cigarettes and motorcycle exhaust—I realize… I make her happy.

It's me that makes her smile.

Just my presence. Just bein' here. Just showin' up when she calls.

I light somethin' up in her that's been dimmin', and I don't know if that makes me her salvation or her damnation, but I know it's true.

"Legion." My name in her mouth sounds pretty today. "Thank you for coming."

I nod. Don't trust my voice.

She gestures to the backdrop—seamless black rollin' down from the ceiling, spotless and pure, waitin' to be filled with whatever image she's got in mind. "Stand there for me?"

I nod.

The time for candid shots is over. She's been done with the stolen moments captured through telephoto lenses from two hundred yards away for years now. She's over the secret documentation of a feral boy she's been stalkin' since he was too young to understand what her attention meant.

She wants to make some art.

She wants to turn me into art.

She wants to photograph me properly. Wants to create somethin' intentional instead of somethin' stolen.

Wants my permission, my participation, my presence as her subject instead of her prey.

I get it. When I'm here. When I'm with her, it really does all make sense.

So I walk to the backdrop without question. Step onto the black. Turn to face her.

This is the only thing she wants from me. The only gift I can give her. My body as her subject. My presence as her art. The chance to create beauty out of the broken Kane boy nobody else sees.

Eleanor lifts her camera and begins directin' me.

"Turn this way." Her voice is soft. Professional. "Lift your chin just slightly. Good. Now look at the light—not at me, at the light."

I follow her instructions. Every word a command I obey without hesitation.

"Take off your jacket."

I shrug out of the leather. Let it fall.

"Your shirt."

I pull the black t-shirt over my head. Stand there bare-chested, tattoos on display—the biblical war inked across my back and arms, the tally marks near my collarbone that nobody asks about, all the evidence of violence and devotion permanently marked into my skin.

Eleanor's breath catches. "Beautiful," she whispers. Then, louder—"Turn around. Slowly."

I turn. Let her see the descent of angels on my shoulder blades, the chain-binder demon down my spine, all the mythology I've wrapped myself in like armor against a world that decided I was damned before I learned to walk.

The shutter clicks. Once. Twice. Over and over, the sound punctuatin' the silence between us like a heartbeat, like breath, like the rhythm of creation itself.

"Face me again."

I do.

"Your jeans. You can leave the rest, but—"

I unbuckle my belt. Unbutton. Unzip. Push denim and boxer-briefs down together and step out of everything, standin' completely naked on back paper under hot lights while Eleanor Ashby—mother of the girl I've been fuckin' in secret since we were teenagers—photographs every inch of me.

No shame. No hesitation. Just givin' her what she needs.

The shutter clicks. Methodical and professional. Eleanor workin' with the precision of someone who's done this ten-thousand times, who knows exactly what angle catches light best, what pose reveals truth instead of hidin' it.

She circles me. Captures me from every direction. Every line. Every scar. The tattoos. The muscle. The evidence of hard labor and harder livin'. Everything.

I stand any way she wants me. Patient. Present. Lettin' her create whatever she needs to create.

Minutes pass. Maybe an hour. Time stops meanin' anything under the lights, with the shutter clickin', with Eleanor hummin' softly to herself the way artists do when they're lost in their work.

Finally, she lowers the camera.

Satisfied. Complete. Whatever she came here to capture, she got it.

"Thank you," she says, and there's tears in her eyes

now, though she's still smilin'. "You have no idea what this means to me."

I want to ask why. Want to understand what she sees when she looks at me through that lens. Want to know if she's photographin' Legion Kane or the ghost of my father.

But I don't ask. Just nod. Start pullin' my clothes back on while Eleanor packs up her camera, saves the film, makes notes in a leather-bound journal about exposure settings, and lighting ratios, and whatever technical details matter to her.

And standin' here now in her underground-bunker archive, surrounded by the aftermath of her life's work, I actually do laugh. Because I just realized somethin'.

If Eleanor had been alive when I went to prison, my whole world would've fallen apart.

Because I would've *never* went to prison if Eleanor was here to stop it.

She would've moved heaven and earth to get me off, even if I begged her not to. Would've hired lawyers, called in favors, leveraged every connection the Ashby name carried. Would've made it impossible for me to give up three years of my life to a man who was gonna betray me anyway.

My sacrifice only worked because she was already gone.

That's the only reason I'm here, soaked in dirt that smells like blood.

Because my angel, it turns out, wasn't Savannah Ashby.

It was Eleanor.

Savannah moves to an antique safe built into the

wall. Early 1900s steel, fireproof, surrounded by cinderblocks like it's holdin' nuclear codes instead of photographs.

She knows the combination by heart. Spins the dial, memory guidin' her fingers through the sequence.

The safe door swings open with a heavy metallic groan.

And there it is.

Red leather. Hand-bound. Thirteen by thirteen inches. Five hundred and twelve pages of my life rendered into art by a woman who saw me when nobody else did.

Savannah lifts it out with both hands. Reverent. Careful. Like she's carryin' something sacred that might shatter if she breathes wrong.

She turns and extends it toward me.

I take it.

The weight surprises me—heavier than I remember, thick with paper, and memories, and Eleanor's relentless documentation of a boy who wasn't supposed to matter.

I carry the book to a velvet couch against the far wall and sink down into cushions. Savannah settles beside me, close enough that our shoulders touch.

I open the Book of Legion.

First page: me at maybe two years old. Dust-streaked skin, messy blond hair catchin' sunlight. I'm holdin' a Matchbox car, blue eyes wide and bright, smilin' at somethin' off-camera.

Turn the page and find more of the same. There are no skips in time in this book. Every day, it feels like she was there, takin' my picture.

I grow up before our eyes.

Me at four or five, standin' at the edge of a school playground. Alone. Watchin' other kids play. The composition's perfect—Eleanor caught the isolation, the loneliness, the way even then I stood outside lookin' in.

Me at seven, climbin' a fence. Scraped knees. Torn shirt. But the light—God, the way she captured the light turnin' my hair almost white, makin' me look like somethin' celestial instead of just another throwaway kid nobody wanted.

I'm smilin' now. Can't help it.

Page after page, Eleanor documented moments I forgot existed. Me runnin' through fields. Ridin' that dirt bike I bought at fifteen. Standin' by my motorcycle at sixteen, seventeen, eighteen—always alone, always watchin', always waitin' for somethin' I couldn't name.

Then the pictures shift.

Me and Savannah together.

Fourteen and twelve, sittin' at the silo entrance. Just talkin'. Eleanor must've been hidin' in the trees with a telephoto lens, because we never saw her, never knew we were bein' captured.

Fifteen and thirteen. My arm around Savannah's shoulders. Both of us laughin' at somethin'.

Sixteen and fourteen. The kiss. Our first real kiss, the one Eleanor showed me years later when she came to the garage. But here it's different—not just one shot but an entire sequence. Before. During. After. The way we looked at each other. The way the world disappeared.

Tears start fallin'.

Not sobbin'. Not breakin'. Just water spillin' from

my eyes like my body needs to release somethin' it's been holdin' in for twenty-five years.

I turn to Savannah.

She's cryin' too. Tears so big they fall down her face in streams, catchin' light from the overhead fixture, turnin' her into somethin' otherworldly.

"She loved me," I say, and my voice cracks on the words. "Eleanor loved me."

Savannah nods. Can't speak.

"My mother never took a single picture of me." This truth is somethin' I never allowed myself to acknowledge. That my mother never loved me. Not the way a mother should. "Not one, Savannah. Not one damn picture. All she wanted was to forget who I came from. Forget what Matthias left behind when he disappeared."

I turn another page. Another memory Eleanor preserved.

"But Eleanor was there. Preserving every moment. Like I was worth rememberin'. Like I mattered."

The pages progress. Me at nineteen, twenty, twenty-one. The tattoos spreadin' across my skin like armor, like prophecy, like the visual representation of everything I was becomin'.

Then the studio portraits begin.

Professional shots. Composed. Intentional.

Me shirtless. Back turned. Angels descendin' across my shoulder blades.

Me facin' forward. Chest bare. The war inked into my flesh on full display.

Then me completely naked. Every angle, but instead

of being exposed, I am covered in just the right amount of shadow.

Art made from flesh, and ink, and light.

I blow out a breath and tap the picture. "All these were at her studio in Glendive."

Savannah sniffles. "I didn't even know she had that studio until after she died. It was in the will. I..." She stops to cry for a moment. "I never even went to look at it. I just... had it sold."

Fuck. That's rough. But I have to keep goin'. I can't stop now. "All she wanted was to turn me into art. To see somethin' beautiful in what everyone else called trash. And I let her. Because for one hour, standin' under those lights while she worked—I got to be more than Legion Kane. More than the demon. More than the curse.

"She loved my father," I say. The words come easier now, like confession. "Matthias Kane. He rode through Drybone in the late nineties with the Sons of Dust. Eleanor loved him. Wanted him. But he chose my mother instead. The waitress with nothin' to offer except herself." I look at Savannah. "Why? Why the hell would anyone choose her over your mother?"

Savannah's hand finds mine, gives me a squeeze. "Well, I'm not sure, Legion. But I bet that Marcus White Jr. has been askin' himself that very same question for the better part of three months now."

I actually chuckle at that. "Yeah. I bet that son-of-a-bitch is. My mama got pregnant. And then Matthias left her. Left everyone, because he didn't really leave, he was dead. Eleanor never forgot him. Never stopped lookin' for him in every shadow, every stranger. And then... she found me."

I tap the picture again.

"This book was supposed to be mine. Eleanor tried to give it to me a dozen times. But I refused. Told her it would get lost. Ruined. That I didn't deserve her art, couldn't honor it the way it deserved."

I look at Savannah.

"I told her to keep it safe. To hide it somewhere nobody could destroy it."

My voice drops to barely a whisper.

Then I actually laugh. "She hid it in a fuckin' bomb shelter."

Savannah laughs too.

I turn another page. Find the last photograph in the book. The selfie. Eleanor and me in a truck, summer sun blazin', both of us smilin' genuine smiles. I remove it from the book and look at Savannah. "We did have a secret, though."

She sucks in a breath, afraid of what I'm gonna say.

But I say it anyway. Holding up the photo. "She was dyin', Savannah. A month before we took this road trip, she was diagnosed with pancreatic cancer."

Savannah gasps. "What? What are you talkin' about? She didn't die of cancer! She had a..."

She doesn't finish. She doesn't have to.

Eleanor Ashby had no intention of goin' out *dyin'*.

She had no intention of wasting away to some shell of her former self.

And Savannah knows this.

"I was takin' her to the Mayo Clinic for treatment.

We only went three times. Then she just said… fuck it. I try to talk her out of givin' up. I did. I didn't want her to die. But she was done. And, in the end, I had to respect that. That's what we were doing in this pic. I was her friend. She was my friend and I was taking her to the hospital."

And now, I'm really fuckin' crying. Because I've never had the chance to tell anyone about how much I loved Eleanor.

Hell, I never even told myself how much I loved her.

But everything is over now. I've got nothing left. Just dead bodies in the blood red dirt.

I blow out a breath, collect myself, then pull out the old, weathered envelope I dug up from the ground out on our twenty acres of scrubland.

I hand it to her. She takes it, not knowing why.

"Read it," I tell her.

So she does.

Dear Legion,

I failed the man I loved. Let me not fail his son.

You think Brick Ransom is your savior. He is not. He is a predator who feeds on boys who remind him of what he could never become. Your father blazed too bright, too wild, and Brick extinguished him because men like Brick cannot tolerate beauty they cannot possess.

Matthias rode into Drybone with fire in his veins and poetry in his fists. He made me believe in resurrection. Then Brick murdered him in cold blood and called it a necessity. Badlands swallowed the lie whole.

Now Brick watches you the same way he watched your

father—with hunger masquerading as brotherhood. He sees Matthias in your shoulders, your silence, your refusal to bow. It enrages him. It always has.

He will destroy you, Legion. Not quickly. Not cleanly. He will hollow you out from the inside, make you complicit in your own erasure, then discard what remains when you no longer amuse him.

Leave Montana. Leave before Brick makes you another tally mark in his decades-long war against everything your father represented.

Run, sweet boy. Run before he buries you beside the only man I ever loved.

—E.

E.

S.

They signed their letters the same way. A single letter. It says everything.

Savannah looks at me. "Brick…"

I nod. "He killed my father. I've known this for seven years. And this morning… I killed him. "

"What?" Her lips form the word, but no sound comes out.

I pull the letter from Savannah's hands and set it on the steel table beside Eleanor's red book. The paper's edges are soft from years folded in my wallet, then buried in Montana clay, then dug back up tonight before I rode here.

I tell her about the Feds. The nomads who weren't nomads. Brick's deal that turned forty-seven brothers into informants over two years while I sat in Whitefall, keeping my mouth shut about crimes that never fuckin' mattered.

I tell her about the fine. Twenty-five thousand dollars I couldn't pay. The bag of money under my pillow with a note that said *got you tomorrow*—bait I took anyway because I needed to see who'd try to buy me.

I tell her about church this morning. The gun. Brick's head. The nomads. Havoc's death.

Thirty-five people in nine holes twelve feet deep.

Savannah doesn't speak. Doesn't move. Just watches me with those blue eyes that used to look at me like I could be saved.

I watch her face for disgust. Horror. The moment she understands what I am.

But she stays still. Listening. Present.

Like she already knew.

Maybe she did. Maybe Eleanor told her in ways I'll never understand. Maybe Savannah saw it the first time we met at the silo when I was fourteen—saw the mark already written on me in ink that wasn't even there yet.

My damnation was signed the day Matthias Kane rode through Drybone, fucked a waitress, and disappeared.

Sealed when Eleanor found me as a baby burning with fever and decided I looked like the ghost she couldn't stop loving.

Finalized when Brick put a bullet in my father's skull and waited thirty-two years for the chance to do the same to his son.

I am Legion.

The demons inside the swine.

And we will *never* have a happy ending.

I stand. Savannah's hand reaches for mine but I'm already moving toward the elevator. The doors slide open. I step inside.

She doesn't follow me.

Good. Because it's over now.

It's truly over now—not just between us, but everything. The whole rotten structure I thought was brotherhood.

Badlands is about to turn into Ruby Ridge. Waco. Every fucking FBI siege they ever televised, every bloody standoff that ended with bodies in bags and ATF agents testifying in front of Congress.

I think about the war etched across my back and chest—angels descending to hunt demons, demons rising to drag them down, an eternal battle that never ends because neither side can win.

Except that's bullshit.

The angels never had a fucking chance.

This world doesn't belong to heaven. Never did. It belongs to the legions—the many, the numbered, the marked. We're born into it screaming and we die choking on our own blood.

Everything in between is just distance between graves.

Good tries.

God knows, it *tries*.

But trying doesn't mean shit when the dirt remembers every body buried in it, and the rain keeps washing blood into the river, and the river keeps flowing toward the same black ocean.

The demons won before the first word was spoken.

Before light.

Before anything clean existed to be ruined.

We just keep pretending otherwise.

Because the alternative is admitting we were fucked from the start.

FBI BOOK CLUB — FINAL SESSION
Assignment:
The Book of Legion (Book of Legion #5) by JA Huss
Transcript — CLASSIFIED
(This time Castillo isn't insisting. This time it actually is.)

[8:47 AM — AGENT: KOWALSKI has started the meeting]
[8:47 AM — AGENT: KOWALSKI has flagged meeting as: EMERGENCY — LEVEL BLACK]

[KOWALSKI VISUAL — bedroom floor, mascara destroyed, empty wine bottle, book facedown on chest like a defibrillator]

Kowalski: I am calling this meeting thirteen minutes early because I have been on this floor since 4 AM and I am NOT getting up. I'm not going to work. I'm not filing reports. I am tendering my resignation from the

Federal Bureau of Investigation to become an old lady at the nearest MC and if anyone has a problem with that you can find me facedown in Montana clay next to thirty-six fucking bodies because THAT'S WHERE MY HEART LIVES NOW. 💀🖤⚔️💧😰🔪🪦💀🖤⚔️💧😰🔪😰

[8:48 AM — AGENT: MARSH has entered the meeting]
[MARSH VISUAL — indoor range, both hands on Glock]

Marsh: I've been here since five. Four magazines. Two for Brick. One for Cash. One for myself because I am a licensed psychologist who has spent five weeks building a clinical profile on a fictional morally gray MMC with a demon name and I just need to sit with what I've become.

[8:48 AM — AGENT: DAVID has entered the meeting]
[DAVID VISUAL — office, blinds drawn, tie missing, collar open, eyes red]

David: Before we begin, I want to establish that I am fine.

Kowalski: You look like a man who finished a dark romance at 3 AM and hasn't recovered. You look like the BEFORE photo in a book hangover post.

David: I said I'm fine. Not that I slept.

[8:49 AM — AGENT: KAI has entered the meeting]
[KAI VISUAL — predawn darkness, headlamp on, vast empty Montana landscape, distant compound lights in background]

Kowalski: Kai. KAI. Are those compound lights behind you?

Kai: I'm not confirming or denying my current location.

Kowalski: YOU'RE STILL IN FUCKING MONTANA. 😮‍💨⚔️💀💧

Kai: I have a lot of PTO.

[8:49 AM — AGENT: CASTILLO has entered the meeting]
[CASTILLO VISUAL — her usual office. Clean desk. No files. No suspect. No second monitor with Google Earth. Hands folded. Face blank.]

Kowalski: Castillo?

[silence]

Kowalski: ...OK we're starting. HE KILLED BRICK. Legion walked into church with a Glock and shot Brick point blank between the FUCKING eyes and I have never felt more SEEN by a fictional man in my entire life. He didn't hesitate. He didn't monologue. He just — BANG — and then Diesel and Chains and Ratchet opened up because they KNEW. They were fucking

WAITING for him to pull the trigger. Ride or die is not a trope in this book it's a LIFESTYLE and I am 💀🖤⚔️💧🥵🔪😭▢💀💀💀 — I need to be picked up off this floor. Somebody send help. I am FERAL. I am in my FINAL FORM—

David: The church sequence is—

Kowalski: Do NOT make this formal, David. HAVOC. Havoc took three fucking bullets and kept fighting. Havoc who GRILLS RIBS. Havoc who has SIX KIDS. Havoc who sat at that dinner table talking about the backside of twenty-three with June and — 💀💀💀💀💀 — JUNE. Oh my God, June is at that farmhouse right now and she doesn't KNOW—

Marsh: The Havoc death is — [magazine release, reload, slide rack] — listen, I had a whole attachment theory framework prepared for this session and I'm throwing it out because FUCK the framework. He was the only functional relationship model in five books. He showed Legion what love looks like after twenty-three years and then he bled out on the church floor three chapters later. That's not character development, that's an ASSASSINATION of my emotional stability. [GUNFIRE — 2 rounds]

Kowalski: MARSH SAID FUCK. THE BOOK BROKE MARSH. 💀💀💀💀💀

David: Castillo — thirty-six bodies, burial logistics,

Montana clay density. You tracked a grain elevator by satellite in session one. Thoughts?

[silence]

David: Castillo?

[silence]

Castillo: No.

Kowalski: She — what? One word? CASTILLO. There is a MASS GRAVE. You GPS'd a fictional clubhouse. You made a suspect cry during our Book 3 discussion. And NOW you have nothing?

Castillo: Continue.

Kowalski: Castillo not talking is scarier than anything in this book and this book has a mass burial. 😩⚔️💀🩸🔪

Marsh: Selective mutism in a previously hyper-verbal subject is actually—

Castillo: I'm fine. Continue.

Kowalski: THE ENDING. He rides to Savannah COVERED in dirt from burying thirty-six people. Covered in it. Montana clay under his nails, in his hair, ground into the brand scar on his chest. And he takes her to Eleanor's vault and shows her the Book of Legion and he CRIES.

This man. This touch-her-and-die, property-of, morally gray, down-bad-since-fourteen, only-her-for-eighteen-years man with twenty-seven dollars and a demon name — he looks at photos of himself as a TODDLER that his own mother never bothered to take and he breaks. He fucking BREAKS. Because a complicated dead woman loved him when nobody else did.

David: And then he tells Savannah everything. The shootout. Brick. The informants. The bodies. All of it.

Kowalski: And then he STANDS UP. Walks to the elevator. And LEAVES HER IN THE VAULT. Alone. Because he thinks the demons won.

DNR. Do not resuscitate. Bury me in the vault next to Eleanor's photographs. I am DECEASED.

Marsh: OK from a clinical — no, fuck it, I'm not doing clinical. The man exhibits textbook avoidant-dismissive attachment with — [GUNFIRE — 3 rounds] — no, I said FUCK the framework. He WALKED AWAY. After everything. After she chose him over her inheritance, her family, her four million followers, her entire curated existence. After she literally got PROPERTY OF DEMON tattooed on her body and rode for him in front of forty-seven bikers and—

Kowalski: ...👀
Kai: ...👀
Castillo: ...👀
David: ...👀

Marsh: Anyway his abandonment schema clearly replicates the original maternal—

Kowalski: SHE DIAGNOSED HERSELF AND WENT RIGHT BACK TO DIAGNOSING LEGION I AM SCREAMING 💀💀💀💀💀

Marsh: I'm a professional, Kowalski. I can be unhinged AND clinical. [GUNFIRE — 1 round] That one was for Legion walking away.

David: I need to discuss something.

Kowalski: We're DISCUSSING—

David: Not about Legion. About Brandy.

[silence]

David: He shot her. She walked toward him with her phone and he didn't even — she was twenty-one. She had this way of standing on that porch watching everything and I — I read her as someone trapped. I thought underneath the handler bullshit there was a person who was in over her head and—

Kowalski: David.

David: What.

Kowalski: Did you claim Brandy as your book girlie?

David: I found her narratively compelling.

Marsh: ...👀
Kowalski: ...👀
Kai: ...👀
Castillo: ...👀

David: Don't do that.

Kowalski: David. DAVID. You defended Marcus for forty-five minutes in session one. You found the federal plant who leaked sex tapes "narratively compelling." You have a TYPE and that type is "red flag factory with a smile." You are the toxic woman magnet. You are the man who looks at a burning building and says "but what if I could FIX the fire."

Marsh: That's actually — yeah, no, she's right. Attraction to emotionally unavailable women who present controlled surfaces while actively undermining — David, you need to be on my couch IMMEDIATELY.

David: I don't need to be—

Marsh: You fell for a FED PLANT in a BIKER COMPOUND in a BOOK, David. You need SO much couch time. Your attachment pattern is "she'll ruin my life and I'll write a report about it." That's not a love language, that's a fucking DIAGNOSIS. [GUNFIRE — 1 round]

Kowalski: 💀 💀 💀 💀 💀 💀 💀 💀 💀 MARSH IS SHOOTING AND DIAGNOSING AT THE SAME TIME. This book club has become a crime scene.

David: SHE WAS TWENTY-ONE AND THEY PLANTED HER IN A COMPOUND FULL OF DANGEROUS MEN AND NOBODY TALKS ABOUT WHAT THAT COSTS—

Kowalski: OH MY GOD HE'S DEFENDING HER. He's doing the Marcus thing again but for BRANDY. He's pulling a Book 1 David. Someone stop this man from falling in love with villains.
Kai: David. She was a handler. She knew what the job was.

David: You don't KNOW—

Kai: I know what handlers look like. I'm standing near where they buried hers.

Marsh: ...👀
Kowalski: ...👀
David: ...👀
Castillo: ...👀

Kowalski: The way I just got full body chills from that sentence. 😩 💀 🖤 ⚔️ Kai hasn't raised his voice ONCE in five sessions and every single thing he says hits like a fucking freight train—

[9:01 AM — KAI's phone buzzes audibly on camera]
Kai: Hold on.

Kowalski: What?

Kai: I just got a text from headquarters.

David: We're in the middle of—

Kai: Holy shit… I've been reassigned. Permanently. Effective immediately. Prairie Division. Montana field office.

David: There IS no Montana field office in Prairie Division.

Kai: There is now. It's a decommissioned gas station outside Terry

David: …👀
Marsh: …👀
Kowalski: …👀

Kai: Castillo.

[silence]

Kai: How long have you known?

[long silence]

Castillo: Three weeks.

Kowalski: WHAT THE FUCK— 😩⚔️💀💧🔪😣💀

Castillo: They briefed me three weeks ago. Kai's reassignment. The field office. All of it. They've been reading our transcripts since session two. The coordinates I provided were logged as preliminary field intelligence. My "hobby" was reclassified as active casework. Retroactively.

David: That's why IA flagged us.

Castillo: IA didn't flag us, David. IA was told to WATCH us. Different thing.

Kowalski: You — FIVE WEEKS. Five weeks you sat here letting us think you were just a psycho reader who happened to GPS fictional crime scenes and you were ACTUALLY WORKING A CASE?? 💀💀💀💀💀💀💀💀

Castillo: I was doing both. But the reason I'm not talking today is because I couldn't discuss the reassignment until it went official. It went official four minutes ago. And I need you all to listen to me very carefully. SEASON TWO OF BADLANDS MC IS… I can't even talk about it. Literally. Classified. But even if it wasn't, I just… can't.

Kowalski: Legion. 😩🖤💀

Castillo: When Legion buried those bodies, he didn't close a case file. He opened one.

David: Our next assignment—

Castillo: Classified.

David: I'm the moderator of this—

Castillo: David. You fell in love with a dead Fed. You are in no position to demand clearance.

Kowalski: 💀 💀 💀 💀 💀 💀 💀 💀 💀 💀 CASTILLO JUST KILLED DAVID WITH WORDS. Five weeks of silence was WORTH IT for that one sentence. I am adding Castillo to my book boyfriend list. I don't care that she's a woman. She has the most devastating one-liner energy of any character in this entire operation.

David: I did NOT fall in—

Kowalski: You DID. And she's RIGHT. And I need everyone on this call to understand that I am permanently altered. I walked into this book club a functioning federal agent with a 401k and I'm walking out a woman who's only goal is to be an old lady in a MC. And if I have to drive to a decommissioned gas station in Terry, Montana and sit in it with Kai until season two drops to prove my attachment to a fictional man — I will.

Kai: ...I'll leave the coffee on.

[9:07 AM — AGENT: KOWALSKI has ended the meeting]

[9:07 AM — AGENT: DAVID (text to group chat):] For the record, I did not fall in love with Brandy. I recognized narrative complexity. These are different things.

[9:08 AM — AGENT: KOWALSKI (text to group chat):] David, baby, that IS love. 🖤

[9:08 AM — AGENT: CASTILLO (text to group chat):] Pack a bag, Kowalski. Terry gets cold in March.

[9:09 AM — AGENT: MARSH (text to group chat):] Requesting transfer to Prairie Division. For professional reasons. Not the book. [attached: Transfer_Req_Prairie_Div.pdf]**

[9:09 AM — AGENT: KAI (text to group chat):] Gas station has room for five.

[END TRANSCRIPT — RECLASSIFIED: ACTIVE OPERATION FILE]

END OF BOOK SHIT

Welcome to the End of Book shit. This is the part of the book where I get to say anything I want about the book you just read. Thoughts about what was on my mind, my plans, how it turned out, why I wrote it—stuff like that.

If you just read that FBI Book Club and you're wondering what the fuck that was — welcome. That little bit of insanity was born right here in this series. Nowhere else. It started as a joke in my newsletter about having my own FBI agent assigned to me because of my "professional research" and it grew legs and a security clearance and apparently a decommissioned gas station in Terry, Montana. I don't know where it's going. I don't think Kowalski does either. But Castillo has a plan and I've learned not to ask questions when Castillo has a plan.

Now. Let's talk about what just happened to you.

You finished. You're sitting there. Maybe it's 2 AM. Maybe it's noon on a Tuesday and you're supposed to be somewhere. You're staring at nothing. Your chest feels like someone parked a truck on it. You might be on the floor. You might have texted someone WHO HASN'T EVEN READ THE SERIES and just said "I need you to know I'm not OK" and they said "what happened" and you said "a fictional man walked into an elevator" and they said "what" and you said "I CAN'T EXPLAIN IT JUST HOLD ME."

That, my friends, is a book hangover.

And unlike the cliffhanger — which I covered in a very scholarly and historically accurate blog post — the book hangover doesn't come from the story stopping.

It comes from the story ending and YOU not being able to.

The story is done with you. You are not done with it. It has moved into your chest like an uninvited guest and it is not paying rent and it knows where you sleep.

This is not new. This is ancient. Allow me to present the evidence…

Murasaki Shikibu, circa 1021 AD. When *The Tale of Genji* — widely considered the first novel ever written — reached the court ladies of Heian Japan, there are accounts of women refusing to attend court duties for days after finishing it. One lady-in-waiting supposedly told the Empress she couldn't dress her because "Genji is dead and nothing matters." The Empress reportedly said "He isn't real." The lady-in-waiting reportedly said "Then why are YOU crying?" No formal discipline was recorded. The Empress never denied the tears.

• • •

Samuel Richardson, 1748. After the publication of *Clarissa*, a novel so devastating it runs over a million words and ends exactly the way you're afraid it will, readers across England wrote to Richardson begging him to change the ending. One woman in Bath wrote that she had not left her house in six days because "the world outside does not contain Clarissa and therefore holds nothing for me." Richardson wrote back. His letter said, in its entirety: "Madam, the world outside never did." Historians call this the first recorded author not giving a fuck. I call him a kindred spirit.

The Brontë Problem, 1847-1848. Between *Jane Eyre* and *Wuthering Heights*, the Brontë sisters essentially carpet-bombed England with book hangovers within a twelve-month window. A London bookseller reportedly kept smelling salts behind the counter. One woman returned three days in a row to reread the same chapter in the shop because she refused to purchase the book and "give that woman the satisfaction." A vicar in Yorkshire wrote to his bishop that "weights of an invisible nature are pressing upon the women of this parish" and requested guidance. The bishop did not reply. He was on chapter thirty-one.

Daphne du Maurier, 1938. When *Rebecca* was published, du Maurier's publisher received a letter from a woman who said she'd finished the book four days prior and had since redecorated her entire parlor because "nothing in this room looks the way it did before that ending." Her husband wrote a separate letter asking if the publisher could "please send whatever the next book is, immediately, as my wife has painted the dining room twice and I fear for the upstairs."

Me, 1986. I was sixteen years old sitting on a plane and I met a biker. Not a weekend warrior. Not a Harley cosplayer. A biker. And somehow — in the way that things happened in 1993 that would get everyone arrested today — I ended up on a road trip to the Harley-Davidson factory in York, Pennsylvania with him and his friend.

Not on a bike.

In a white van.

I was sixteen. In a white van. With two bikers I met on a plane.

And I didn't even die.

I tell you this because people ask me where Legion comes from. Where the MC world comes from. Why it feels like I've been in those rooms, smelled that leather, heard the way a clubhouse goes quiet when the wrong person walks in.

Because I grew up adjacent to it. Northeastern Ohio in the 1980s. Lake Erie cold and rust-belt mean. I was a kid sitting on the edges of a world that wasn't mine but left its fingerprints all over me. Men who were terrifying on Friday and coaching Little League on Saturday. Women who stayed — not because they were trapped, but because they looked at the fire and said *mine.*

And then at sixteen, a white van to Pennsylvania, and I came back with a story I've been carrying for over thirty years and only now figured out how to write.

That's what a book hangover really is. It's not about the book. It's about the thing the book unlocked in you that was already there. Legion walking into that elevator, covered in dirt, believing the demons won — that wrecked you because you've watched someone walk away. Or you've been the one walking. Or you've stood in the vault and watched the elevator doors close and known, KNOWN, that the person leaving was wrong about themselves and you couldn't make them see it.

That's Savannah right now.

Standing in Eleanor's archive. Surrounded by photographs of the man she chose. Listening to the elevator rise without her.

She's got a book hangover too.

Only hers hasn't ended yet.

So. What's next. First of all, don't miss the teaser after the EOBS for my next new series in 2026 - MAFIA ROMANCE!

The Book of Legion Season One — all five novellas — will release as an omnibus in ebook, paperback, and AUDIOBOOK in late July or early August 2026.

The audiobook is narrated in duet by **Teddy Hamilton** and **Samantha Summers** and should clock in at around **16 hours**. If you know, you know. If you don't know — Teddy Hamilton voicing Legion is going to be a federal emergency and I'm not even a little sorry about it.

Season Two of the Badlands MC — five more novellas, same weekly release format — will hit in **late August 2026.**

I'm not going to tell you what happens in season two. I'm not going to tell you if Savannah goes after him. I'm not going to tell you if the government comes. I'm not going to tell you what June does when she finds out about Havoc. I'm not going to tell you if Castillo's field office in Terry has a coffee maker.

I will tell you this: the elevator goes both ways.

Thank you for reading, thank you for reviewing, and I'll see you in the next book.

Julie

JA Huss

February 14, 2026

Her CHAINS Her CHOICE

New York Times Bestselling Author

JA HUSS

Last to Fall Book 1

ABOUT THE AUTHOR

JA Huss is a scientist, New York Times and USA Today bestselling author. Her self-published romantasy Sparktopia was named an Audible Editors' Best of the Year selection in 2024, and several of her audiobooks have been nominated for the Audie and SOVA Awards. A 2019 RITA finalist, Huss has also had five books optioned for film and television.

www.ingramcontent.com/pod-product-compliance
Lightning Source LLC
Chambersburg PA
CBHW021350060726
47591CB00006B/2254